SEARCHANDDESTROY

D0097702

Also by Dean Hughes
Soldier Boys

SEARCH
AND
DESTROY

Dean Hughes

GINEE SEO BOOKS
ATHENEUM BOOKS FOR YOUNG READERS
NEW YORK LONDON TORONTO SYDNEY

SOMERSET CO. LIBRARY
BRIDGEWATER, N.J 08807

Atheneum Books for Young Readers • An imprint of Simon & Schuster Children's Publishing Division • 1230 Avenue of the Americas • New York, New York 10020 • This book is a work of fiction. Any references to historical events, real people, or real locales are used fictitiously. Other names, characters, places, and incidents are products of the author's imagination, and any resemblance to actual events or locales or persons, living or dead, is entirely coincidental. • Copyright © 2005 by Dean Hughes • All rights reserved, including the right of reproduction in whole or in part in any form. • Book design by Sonia Chaghtzbanian • The text for this book is set in Garth Graphic. • Manufactured in the United States of America • First Edition • 10 9 8 7 6 5 4 3 2 1 • Library of Congress Cataloging-in-Publication Data • Hughes, Dean, 1943- • Search and destroy / Dean Hughes.—1st ed. • p.   cm. • "Ginee Seo Books." • Summary: Recent high-school graduate Rick Ward, undecided about his future and eager to escape his unhappy home life, joins the army and experiences the horrors of the war in Vietnam. • ISBN-13: 978-0-689-87023-1 (ISBN 13) • ISBN-10: 0-689-87023-X • 1. Vietnamese Conflict, 1961–1975—Juvenile fiction. [1. Vietnamese Conflict, 1961–1975—Fiction. 2. War—Fiction.] I. Title. • PZ7.H87312Se   2006 • [Fic]—dc22 • 2005011255

For my grandson, Michael Russell

ACKNOWLEDGMENTS

I am not a veteran of the Vietnam War. I have, however, spent several years researching and writing about the war and the sixties era. Two men who did fight in Vietnam have read my manuscripts and guided me in making the war material authentic. I'm thankful to Major Richard N. Jeppesen, USMC (Ret), and Lieutenant Colonel Jeffrey C. Berry, U.S. Army (Ret), for their meticulous help.

CHAPTER 1

RICK WANTED TO WIN. HE WATCHED AS THE VOLLEYBALL FLOATED over the net and dropped toward the sand. A teammate in the middle got low and dug the ball, and then Renny set it, very high. Rick loped forward, leaped, then spiked the ball hard with his palm. But he'd mistimed his jump and didn't get over the top of the ball. It shot toward a player on the backline, but the guy jumped aside and let it go. The ball hit beyond the line and all the players on that side of the net cheered.

"That's all right!" he shouted. "You got us that time, but it won't happen again."

"Rick!" Judy was walking toward him. "I told you, I have to go," she said.

"Can't you just wait for one more game?"

"*No!* That's what you said after the last one."

Rick turned to Renny. "Sorry, man. Gotta run."

"Don't worry about it." Renny grinned. "We're better off without you."

"Hey, what are you talking about? I'm your star." Rick gave Renny a fake slam across the chest with his forearm. Renny, who was about four inches shorter than Rick and not as strongly built, acted as though he'd taken a real blow. He stumbled backward, letting his arms fly out, like some sort of clown.

"Okay, maybe *you* don't care if I leave, but what about all these girls longing to gaze at my bronzed physique?" Rick struck a muscleman pose, and Jill Rush laughed appreciatively, then pretended to pant, like a dog.

"Or maybe it's your empty head they like the most," Judy said.

The words had a little too much edge. Rick started to say something, but Judy was already walking away. "Please, Rick. Come on." She didn't even look back.

"Okay, okay." Rick ran across the beach to the spot where he'd left his bag and pulled on his shorts. His boat shoes were full of sand, but he worked his feet into them anyway and ran to catch up with Judy. She'd told him from the beginning that she couldn't stay at the party long. But lately it seemed she was making far too many cracks like the one about his empty head. Actually, Rick thought he was smarter than Judy. True, she got better grades than he did, but she studied night and day. He'd never killed himself on his schoolwork. Still, he read a lot more than she did. Of course, Rick had to admit, she was going places and he wasn't. The two had graduated a couple of weeks before from Millikan High in Long Beach, California, class of 1969. In the fall Judy would be heading to Cal, Berkeley, which was more than Rick could say he was doing. Rick wanted to get away from home too, but he hadn't yet figured out how he was going to do it.

Judy got into the car before Rick could open the door for her, so Rick walked around to the driver's side and tossed his bag on the backseat. He'd worked hard the summer before to buy a '57 Chevy, a two-tone job in turquoise and white. It was his dream car, but it was also falling apart, and he didn't have the money to do much about it. He was working again this summer, making three bucks an hour carrying hod for a bricklayer. At that rate he would bring in a lot of money, but he knew he couldn't put it all into his car if he wanted to go to college in the fall.

"Hey, what's with you lately?" he asked. He felt around in his pockets and realized his keys were in the bag in the backseat.

"What's with *you* lately? I can't believe how serious you are about volleyball."

"Hey, if I'm going to play, I might as well play to win."

She let her eyes roll and then looked away.

"Come on, Judy. What's the matter? You treated

people like garbage today. Are you in a bad mood again or—"

"I'm tired, Rick. We're out of high school and none of your friends act like it."

She was so serious. Judy had an easy smile and soft lips, perfect teeth, but lately she'd stopped wearing makeup, even lipstick, and she hardly seemed to smile anymore. She had started looking like a hippie, with her bell-bottom jeans and her peace beads. The thing was, Judy could look beautiful when she wanted to. So why didn't she want to?

Rick started his car and the radio blasted out Marvin Gaye singing, "I Heard It Through the Grapevine." It was a song he loved, but he turned the radio down. Judy had started listening to nothing but folk music and protest songs. That was all she seemed to care about anymore.

"Listen, Judy. My friends may like to have a good time, but they're not stupid. They're planning to go to college—most of them, anyway."

"*Junior* college, if they get that far."

"Oh, okay. And you got into Berkeley, so all of a sudden you're too high and mighty to hang out with them."

"Shut up, okay?"

"Why should I? You know it's true. You think you're better than everyone else."

"No, I don't. What I'm doing—or at least trying to

do—is grow up. But you—it looks like your only goal is to be as tan as possible and win stupid volleyball games."

Rick didn't know how to respond to that. Didn't she know he was kidding around? When had she lost her sense of humor? He drove for a time before he said, "Look, it's summer. I just want to have fun for a few more months. Then I'm going to . . . you know . . . get going on my goals."

"What goals? You didn't even *apply* to college. You say you want to be a writer, but you don't write anything."

Rick felt stung. "I *do* write."

"Yeah, in your notebook. Show me one thing you've finished. Even a short story."

"I've finished stories before."

"Only in your creative writing class—because you had to get something in for a grade. You've never written anything if you didn't have to." She had begun to turn the knob on the radio, probably looking for some of that stupid music of hers. If he'd done that in her car—her dad's car, actually—she'd have told him to stop it. Why did he put up with her, anyway? Maybe it was time to break up once and for all. They'd done it several times before, but they'd always ended up back together. The thing was, he could talk to her more easily than anyone he'd ever known. There had been a time when the two of them had talked whole nights away, just trying to figure out the world. But she'd changed.

"I write more than you know about," Rick said, weakly.

"Do you? Do you really?" When he didn't answer, she said, "I don't know who you are anymore, Rick. You've got about ten different people inside you and I only like one of them. I don't know why I end up with the other nine most of the time."

"What are you talking about?"

"When you're around Renny, it's like you never left junior high. He's about as deep as an oil slick."

"He likes to have fun, Judy. Fun, remember? It's something you had a *slight* feel for at one time—before you decided you knew everything."

"See, that's the other thing. You and I both know what's wrong with the world, but you pull back. And then you accuse me of being too serious. You'll talk about problems, but you won't *do* anything about them."

It wasn't the first time he'd heard her say that. But the truth was, even though he agreed with a lot of things Judy said, he was never as sure as she was. It wasn't his job to fix the world. People who knew a lot more than either he or Judy did weren't having much luck at doing it. And what made her think she knew all the answers? "So let's see," he said, after a time. "Which me is the one you like?"

"I'm forgetting. Very fast."

"Come on, Judy. Tell me."

She sighed. "Oh, Rick. You know very well—or you ought to. Remember the Joan Baez concert? Remember afterward? You almost cried, talking about the way so many kids in this world have to suffer."

He did remember that night, and he did know that side of himself. He couldn't look at posters of starving children in Africa without feeling over-whelmed with grief. But what did she expect him to do about it?

"I love the part of you that wants to write," Judy said, this time with some softness in her voice. "You've written some beautiful things. But you never finish. You don't have any discipline."

"That's not true! I don't finish because I don't really know anything. I haven't *seen* anything. I haven't experienced anything *real*."

"So that's why you spend your life at the beach with Renny and the old high school crowd?"

"Lay off, Judy. I'm about finished with that. What I'm thinking is that I'll take off and wander for a while. You know, just work my way around the country. Talk to people. Maybe even find a way to get to Europe or somewhere like that." If he could convince her, maybe he could convince himself.

Judy laughed. "Rick, I'm sorry, but you're becoming more of a joke all the time. You won't do anything like that. You know how much you want rolled-and-pleated upholstery for this stupid car.

You'll work all summer and then spend it on stuff like that. Then you'll take a few classes at a local college and drop out after a term or two. You're going to end up like your dad, working at some job you hate just to put food on the table."

Her words hurt a whole lot more than he wanted her to know. "Oh, yeah, and I guess you'll go up to Berkeley and spend all your time being the queen of the protest movement." He had wanted to sound superior, but the words only sounded snide.

"I *will* be involved in the movement. You know that. But I'm going to study, too. I'm going to law school eventually, and I'm going to fight some of the stupidity going on in this country."

She'd finally settled on a radio station that was playing a Bob Dylan song, "A Hard Rain's A-Gonna Fall." Rick had heard it over and over and it made no sense to him. Of course Judy knew exactly what the song meant. It was all part of this phony thing she was doing now—trying to be angry and *profound*.

"Come on, Judy," he said. "*Everything* is stupid to you these days."

"No, not everything. But look. My dad has enough money to do some good in the world, but he's always buying himself a bigger boat or a fancier car. People are starving to death and my parents don't think a thing about spending twenty dollars each on a single meal!"

"Judy, your dad works hard for what he's got. Give him a break."

She jerked to face him, eyes blazing. "You don't get it, do you? You cry about little kids in Africa, but you don't have the faintest idea of what's going on here at home. America has lost its soul. People think they can buy a few more *things* and then they'll be happy. We consume most of the world's goods, and what do we want? More and more toys to play with."

Actually, he agreed with her—to some extent. But he also knew what it was like to go without, and Judy had never once experienced that. He would never tell her, but the truth was, he hadn't applied to colleges because he didn't have the money—not if he wanted to leave home. His dad had already put him on notice that if he wanted to go to college, he was on his own. He could stick around Long Beach and enroll at a junior college, but Judy would make fun of that, and it wasn't what he wanted either.

He almost wished the army hadn't gone to a lottery system this year. He'd drawn a high number and wouldn't be drafted, but sometimes he toyed with the idea of signing up. It was a ridiculous war to get involved in, and all his friends would call him an idiot if he enlisted when he didn't have to. But the thing was, he was curious about experiencing war. Rick was going to write, but he was going to tell real stories—ones that didn't show off. Rick liked Hemingway, liked that he didn't use a lot of words, and liked the brave heroes in his stories. What he really wanted was to face some hard realities, maybe some danger, and discover from that what he wanted to say. Joseph Conrad had sailed up the Congo and found the heart of darkness. Then he had told the truth. That's what Rick wanted to do. But how could he? He hadn't *found* his own truths. Hemingway didn't make war glamorous or noble, but the guy had learned things from being close to the action.

Rick reached over and turned the radio off, just to get Dylan's annoying voice out of his head. "Well," he said, "I'm glad you've got everything figured out. It's interesting that you care so much about helping people, but you treat my friends like dirt. I guess they're not really people to you."

This actually seemed to stop Judy. She was quiet for a time before she said, "I'm frustrated right now, Rick. Southern Cal is probably the most superficial place on this planet. I want to get out of here, and I want to work with people who *care* about our world. Our friends here are nice. I just have no patience with the way they want to live. But you're different, Rick. You have a good heart. You think. You could use your heart and brain and get involved, but you choose not to, and it makes me crazy."

Rick was finally sick of Judy's condescension.

"Well . . . sorry I'm not what you had in mind," he said.

"I'm sorry too, Rick. I really am."

"But don't call you. You'll call me. Right?"

"There won't be any calls. I can't do this anymore."

So he drove her home. He stopped in front of her house and looked at her. "Good-bye, Judith. It's been wonderful talking to you, but I think I've heard enough."

She stared at him for a few seconds and then she laughed. "You *are* a joke." She got out of the car and slammed the door. There were tears in her eyes, which surprised him.

He shifted into gear, but he didn't release the clutch. He sat for a time, trying to think what he felt. What he wished was that he could hurt—really hurt. He wanted to feel like Henry, from *A Farewell to Arms*, destroyed by the loss of Catherine, the nurse he loved. He wanted to be overwhelmed with emotion, then go home and write all night.

It crossed his mind that he could go back to the beach and hang out with Renny for a while longer, just to feel a little better. But that was pointless—as pointless as calling Jill Rush, who had looked so good in her two-piece swimsuit today. The girl had flirted with him so obviously that he knew she was interested. She had no brains at all, but he wasn't sure he cared about that.

He drove home instead and then slipped off to his

bedroom in the back part of the house. He sat for a time and listened to the radio. To his station. First he listened to Jimi Hendrix with the sound on so loud that he knew he would get a knock on his door pretty soon. Then Dionne Warwick sang "This Girl's in Love with You," and he found himself fighting not to cry. He was twenty different guys, not ten, and he wasn't sure he liked any of them. He switched the radio to a jazz station playing a Thelonious Monk tune, turned the sound low, and got out his notebook.

> *Judy dumped me tonight. I don't blame her. She's right about me. I'm a mess. I'm just drifting. I want to leave home, but I don't dare do it. For one thing, I don't know what Mom and Roxie would do. I feel like I need to be here to protect them. Mom's whole life is just serving my dad. She gets scared if every-thing isn't exactly the way he wants it. If I'm not here, he might start beating on her. And what would that do to Roxie? She's only twelve. But I can't be the one Mom leans on forever, and I'm tired of all the yelling around this place.*
>
> *I wish Judy hadn't changed. She's the only person I ever felt really close to. I love who she was, and I hate who she is now. But I guess she feels the same way about me. I*

understand what she's saying about Renny and those guys. I'm getting so I can't stand them either. What's cool at fourteen doesn't work at eighteen, and they don't get that. But when I try to think what's coming, there's only one thing I know for sure: I've got to go to work in the morning, and I hate my job. That's about as far ahead as I can see. Maybe I'll end up like my dad, like Judy says I will. Maybe I'll never have the guts to break away.

In some ways, though, Judy doesn't understand me at all. I know I'm sort of marking time right now, but I'm not lazy. I just don't know what to write yet. I read Salinger, and I know he knows things. He doesn't have to spell it out; I feel it between all the lines. And Hemingway, he hurt so bad, he just let the pain come out, and that made him a writer. I don't want pain for its own sake; I'm not like that. But I don't feel enough, and I've got to find a way to do that on a deeper level. Then I'll write stuff that will blow Judy away.

But then I wonder: What if I actually have no talent? What if I'm just kidding myself? Maybe I'm more like Renny than I want to admit. The worst part is, I don't know. I never seem to know anything for sure.

Rick sat for a time and thought. What else did he want to say? He read back what he'd written and felt like an idiot.

This stuff is all such high school garbage. I hate it when I feel sorry for myself. I'm going to do something with my life. And then I'm going to go look up Judy and ask her what she ever accomplished with all her causes. When I publish my first novel, I'm going to send her a copy. I'll sign it "With love, from the guy you didn't believe in."

CHAPTER 2

RICK HAD A HARD TIME GETTING OUT OF BED THE NEXT MORNING, but he made it to work on time and he put in his day, even though the eight hours seemed like twenty. The money was good, but the work didn't interest him. He mixed mortar for a crew of three bricklayers and then carried it up scaffolds, climbing with a heavy bucket in one hand. Whenever he had time, he also had to "strike joints," which was using a metal tool to smooth out the drying mortar between the bricks. He sort of liked doing that because it finished off the job and made the brickwork look good, but he usually wasn't at it long before he heard his boss wail, in his nasally voice, "Hey, Rick, we need some more mud up here."

The boss, Darrell, was a moody guy. He could be funny and sort of easygoing at times, but he was a stickler about the "mud" and cussed Rick out at times.

Rick mixed the mortar the same way every time, but Darrell was always telling him it was too wet or a shade too light in color. Rick didn't see how it could be, and he didn't see why Darrell had to get so upset about it, but he never talked back to the guy.

On Thursday of that week Darrell showed up in a bad mood. Before Rick mixed his first batch of mortar, Darrell called for him to help pull down some scaffolding and then rebuild it in a new place. That was fine with Rick, but then Darrell yelled about having to wait because no mortar was ready. There was no way for Rick to speed up the process, except to shovel the sand and cement into the mixer a little faster, and that's what he did, but when he carried up the first batch Darrell told him it was way too wet. He swore at Rick and told him, "This job ain't that hard. Your dad told me you were a good kid, and that's why I took you on, but if you don't know how to count how many shovels of sand to throw in, tell me now and I'll hire me a Mexican who at least knows *uno, dos, tres.*"

"I did count. I put in exactly—"

"It's not just counting. You gotta look at the stuff. By now you oughta be able to see when it ain't right."

For three weeks the guy had been harping on him about counting right, mixing by the right formula, and now it was supposed to be a matter of judgment. Rick held on for a moment, then he said, "Do you want me to add a little more sand into this—"

"No. That'll get the color wrong. Just dump this batch out and go back and mix it right."

So what did that mean? Mix it by the numbers or use his judgment? Rick decided to play it safe. He counted carefully as he shoveled in the mix, but he put in a little less water than the time before. He took a good look at the stuff as he dumped it from the mixer and it seemed about right, so he carried a couple of buckets of it around the corner. Darrell was waiting, smoking a cigarette and talking to the other bricklayers. They were all three built like pro wrestlers, with big arms and shoulders, but Darrell had a big gut on him.

When Rick poured out the mortar on Darrell's board, Darrell started cursing. "That ain't no different from what you brought me last time, Rick. What's wrong with you? I don't have all day to wait around here. Can you do this job or can't you?"

Rick knew he was close to losing control, so he said nothing. He put his hands on his hips and waited to find out what Darrell wanted him to do. But Darrell was losing it too. He stuck his toe under the mortar board and flipped it over, dumping the mud on the ground. "Do I have to come around there and mix the stuff, then carry it to myself?"

"Yeah. I guess maybe you do," Rick said. He turned and walked away, pulling off his gloves as he walked. He needed a job, but he wasn't going to put up with any more of this stuff. He could hear Darrell yelling at him, cursing at him for being a punk and an idiot, but he didn't care. People didn't have to treat each other like that. Dad would be mad about him walking off, but he had taken enough.

What Rick didn't dare do was go home. If he returned early, his mother would ask questions and then his dad would find out. He decided to look for another job, and once he found one, he would tell his parents he had decided to try something else. That wouldn't be so bad. Dad would get the word on what had happened sooner or later, since he saw Darrell now and then, but if Rick had a new job, his dad wouldn't be so upset. So Rick drove to the employment office downtown and filled out some papers, but the woman who took the forms didn't give him much hope. "We've got a lot of young guys like you looking," she said. "I hate to admit it, but the best way is to know someone. Or you can pound the pavement—you know, just put in a lot of applications at stores and various kinds of companies."

Rick had never had to look for a job before. He had always worked during the summer, but usually his dad had known someone, or some friend had told him about an opening. He hadn't realized it was so hard to find work. But he didn't go looking that day. He couldn't really pound on doors dressed the way he was, and that sort of stuff scared him anyway. He thought maybe he'd check around with some of his friends that night, just to see if anyone knew of anything.

He drove over to the beach, ate his lunch, then found some shade and slept for a while. At 4:30, when he normally got off work, he headed home. He took a shower and ate dinner with his parents and little sister, and he didn't say anything about his day. But it wasn't long after dinner that he heard the phone ring and then, soon after, heard his dad's voice. "Hey, Rick, come on out here."

Rick was lying on his bed, reading and listening to the radio. He turned the book over on his bed and got up. "Rick!" he heard again. His dad had first called from down the hallway, but now he was right outside the door. Rick opened the door and saw immediately that his dad was angry. "I just talked to Darrell on the phone. He said you quit your job."

"Yeah, I did."

"What were you *thinking*—or were you just *not* thinking, as usual?"

Dad had probably showered after work, but the grime—even the smell—never seemed to come off him. He was wearing an old plaid shirt with the shirttail hanging out, his big stomach, like Darrell's, bulging underneath. "That guy treats people like dirt, Dad. There was no way I could get anything right for him. He kept swearing at me like I was—"

"So what are you, a cupcake? Can't you take a little

chewing?" Now it was Dad who let out a stream of curses. "Men on the job don't talk like old-maid schoolteachers. If you do something wrong, they tell you—and they give it to you straight."

"Hey, I can take that. But Darrell was on my back from the day I got there. You wouldn't believe some of the stuff he called me."

Dad slammed the palm of his hand against the door frame, shaking the wall. He was not a big guy, not as tall as Rick, but he was powerfully built, and Rick could see how much he wanted to pound his son instead of the wall. He had done plenty of that when Rick was a kid. What he had called spankings had sometimes been more like beatings. He hadn't done that for quite a few years now, but he had seemed on the edge at times, and Rick had never seen him angrier than he was right now. "Get out!" he shouted. "If you think you can pick and choose your job when work is so hard to come by, then go out and make it on your own. I'm not going to feed you anymore."

Rick heard his mother begin to cry. He couldn't see her, but he knew she was down the hall watching all this, scared what her husband might do. Dad turned toward her and shouted, "Just stay out of this, Helen. It's you always spoiling him that's made him like this. If he has to look out for himself, maybe he'll start to act like a man."

"Where's he supposed to go?"

"That's his problem. He's the one who quit his job. I guess maybe he can sell that pretty car he loves so much. That might buy him a little food for a while."

Actually, Rick was relieved. Dad had made the decision for him. Rick was tired of Darrell, but he was a lot more tired of his father, and he had been for a long time. So he walked to his closet and grabbed his gym bag. Then he started throwing jeans and shirts and underwear into it. At that point Dad walked away. The man was probably bluffing, and Mom might talk him out of the whole thing, but Rick had had enough. He felt bad only when Mom came into the room. "Just wait an hour or two. Don't go," she said. "He'll calm down."

Rick looked at her, saw how scared she was. She was a little woman, just turned forty, but she looked older, her light hair already full of gray. Her rounded face was red now, her eyelashes wet. She was holding a dish towel and she used it to dab at her eyes and nose. She was the patient one, the peacemaker, and yet Dad was always calling her ugly names and threatening her—especially when he was drinking.

"Mom, I gotta get out of here. I'm the one who always makes him mad. Things will be easier for you if I'm gone." Rick didn't believe that, but he wanted to. He didn't want to feel as though he were running out on her.

"No, things won't be better for me. But that's not

what I'm worried about. You don't have anything to live on. I don't know what you'll do."

"I can probably stay with Renny for a few days. I'll find another job. I'll get by."

"Just go over to Renny's for the night. By tomorrow I can calm him down. But do look for a job tomorrow. If you have something, he won't be so hard to deal with."

"I know."

She put her arms around him, and Rick hugged her for a moment, but he didn't want that. He didn't like it when she babied him. Dad was right about that part. It was time for him to be a man. He grabbed his notebook and threw it in his gym bag, gave Mom a quick peck on the cheek, and then left. He drove to Renny's, and Renny said it was no problem for him to spend a night or two, if he didn't mind sleeping on the floor.

Rick told him that was okay, but he knew it wasn't anything that was going to work very long. Renny's family had money, and they were nice about throwing parties at their house or having "the gang" over, but Rick couldn't picture them feeding him and putting him up for more than a day or two. All the same, no matter what his mother had said, Rick felt like he had to find a way to avoid going back home.

Rick and Renny spent most of the evening sitting in a booth at a loud, greasy-smelling hamburger place called My Blue Heaven. Some of the other guys were there, all talking about their summer jobs and how much they hated them, so Rick's story made him an instant hero. "He told the jerk where to shove it; then he walked off the job," Renny would say, and everyone would laugh.

Rick liked the story the first time or two Renny told it, but gradually, he began to see how pathetic it was. He knew what Judy would say about him—that he was messing everything up, that he had no direction in his life. And now, if he didn't figure something out, he wouldn't have money to go to school that fall. That night, after Renny was asleep, Rick was miserable on the floor, and worried, so he got up and turned on a little lamp at Renny's desk. He pulled his notebook from his gym bag.

My dad kicked me out today. He was mad because I quit my job. I was glad in a way, because I wanted to get out of my house and have some experiences in the world, but now I don't know how to pull that off. All the guys at My Blue Heaven thought I was a big shot tonight—for telling Darrell off. But it was stupid. I should have found something else first. I talked to my friends and no one knows about any work. Half those guys only have part-time jobs slinging hamburgers or sweeping floors. Something like that isn't going to pay for an apartment. I could sell my car, but how would

I get to work? It's not very likely I could find a job that's on a bus line or something like that.

I hope Mom is all right. I hate to leave her with Dad. I hate to think what's going to happen when Roxie grows up and moves away too. Mom only lives for us.

I don't know if I hate my dad. It seems wrong to say that. But he's a bully and he's stupid. I wish I was proud of him—for something—but I can't think of anything. He goes to work every day, and we've never been broke, but that's about the best I can say about him. When I was little I always wanted him to be proud of me, but he never showed anything like that, not even when I did my best in school and sports and stuff. So I give up. I can't please him and I won't try. I just wish Mom didn't have to get caught in the middle.

I've been trying to go to sleep on Renny's floor, but I'm too worried about everything. There's no way this is going to work. I want to take off and maybe work in some other states, but I'd have to have some money saved up to get started. For now I'd have to find some dump of a place to live, but even then, how could I pay the first month's rent and all the deposits and everything? So that's not going to happen. I keep thinking about things, every which way, and the only idea that makes any sense is joining the army. I said that to Renny tonight and he about lost it. He says I'll end up in Vietnam and he's probably right. That does scare me. But maybe that's what I want. I don't understand this war at all. It seems like we're getting a bunch of guys killed for no reason. But still, maybe it's what I need to do.

Rick stopped and thought about that. The idea was terrifying, but it was also exciting. Maybe it wasn't Hemingway's kind of war, but it *was* war.

Maybe I should go to Vietnam. Maybe I could learn some things. Maybe I need to go over there and find out what I can about myself. I don't want to get killed, but I probably wouldn't, and maybe when I got back, I'd be ready to write. I think I'd have some things to say after something like that. Maybe I need to find my Congo and travel down it until I know what Conrad knew—or discover something else. But I'm not sure. Maybe I couldn't handle it.

I feel like I've jumped off a cliff without thinking about how deep the canyon was. I hope I get up in the morning with some other idea, but I'm thinking tonight, the army might be my only answer.

Rick didn't sleep much that night, and in the morning he left without eating breakfast at Renny's. He didn't want to talk to Renny's parents and have to answer a bunch of questions. All night he had tried to think of other ideas. He even considered going home and telling his dad he was sorry, but that was just going back to the life he had to get out of. So the army still seemed the best thing. He had a few bucks in his pocket, so he got breakfast at a little coffee shop close to the beach, and then he looked up the recruiting office in the phone book, got the address, and was waiting at the door when it opened. The guy who showed up to unlock the door was some kind of sergeant, but Rick wasn't exactly sure what all the different stripes meant.

"Come on in," the man said. He flipped on the fluorescent lights. The little room was lined with shelves, all full of brochures. "I'm Sergeant Cavanaugh," the man said. "What can I do for you?" He was an older guy, maybe in his forties, but he was muscular and trim and his hair was cut "high and tight" like the guys in some of the war movies Rick had seen.

"I'm thinking about joining the army."

"All right. Sit down. What's your name?"

"Rick Ward."

There was a desk at the back of the room. Cavanaugh walked to it, then motioned for Rick to sit on the opposite side. Rick thought it was funny how straight the man stood, and the stiff way he moved around, but that also appealed to him in a way. The sergeant seemed like the real thing—the way a soldier was supposed to be. Everything on the guy's desk was stacked neatly and lined up at right angles. "Tell me this, Ward," Cavanaugh said, "are you a high school graduate?"

"Yeah. I graduated about three weeks ago."

"Good grades?"

"Pretty good."

"What is it you want from the army?"

"I guess I want some new experiences. And I feel like I need some discipline. Maybe I can learn that in the army." Rick had thought about what he might say; he thought that stuff would sound good to a recruiter.

"Do you know about the G. I. Bill?"

"Not exactly."

"After you serve you can get a stipend for college tuition and expenses. If you don't have the cash to start college right now, the G. I. Bill is a good way to go."

"Yeah, I've heard something about that. That makes a lot of sense to me." The truth was, Rick hadn't considered the money for college a factor until this moment, but it was something he could tell his parents. Even Judy. He would have a plan.

"You realize, there's a pretty strong chance you could serve part of your hitch in Vietnam."

"Actually, is there a way to be sure I get to go? That's something I want to do."

Sergeant Cavanaugh was watching Rick closely, almost as though this were a job interview. Rick had expected the man to jump all over him and ask him to start signing papers. "Tell me about that," he said. "Why do you want to serve in Vietnam?"

"Well . . . you know . . . those people have a right to freedom. The Communists shouldn't be coming in there taking over and everything." Rick had actually believed that at one time, but then the war had bogged down and nothing had come of any of that. Still, he figured it was exactly what the sergeant would want to hear.

Cavanaugh showed no reaction. He was studying Rick. "See this?" he finally said. He pointed to a medal above his left pocket—a blue bar with a silver rifle across it. "That's called a CIB—Combat Infantryman Badge. I served a year in Vietnam. So I know what I'm talking about. If you join up thinking you're going to be a hero, you won't find the satisfaction you're looking for. No one back here in the States is going to thank you."

"I'm sure that's right. But I'm just saying, I want to do my part. I was even thinking I might want to get into Special Forces or something like that."

"Young man, I hope you know, war is nothing at all like the movies."

"Sure. I figured that." Rick had seen *The Green Berets*. He and Renny had laughed at all the gung-ho soldiers, but Rick hadn't admitted to Renny that he actually liked the idea of being as tough as those guys—not scared of anything.

"Were you a high school athlete, Ward?"

"Yeah. I played football and I wrestled."

"That'll help you. If you can pass the screening test high enough, and if you handle basic training well, you can apply for Special Forces. You can get yourself a beret, if that's what you want. And you'll like how you feel about yourself. You'll get yourself into great shape, and you'll know you're fighting with the best. But you need to know, you may be raising your chances of getting killed or wounded. I came home with a chunk of shrapnel in my back."

Sergeant Cavanaugh hesitated and watched Rick, and Rick did his best not to blink. The idea of getting killed had seemed remote as Rick had thought about it on Renny's floor last night, but with this man staring at him—a soldier still carrying shrapnel in his body— Rick felt his breath catch in his chest. But there was a certain thrill in the idea too. Dad was always saying that Rick wasn't a man. What would he say when he came home with a badge like that?

"I'm a professional soldier," Sergeant Cavanaugh said. "I'm proud of what I do, but some of these protesters who come around here tell me I entice you boys with lies. So I want to be straight with you. Army training is hard, and Vietnam is the closest thing to hell

I've ever experienced. If you're looking for adventure, this is the wrong way to find it. You're not signing up for summer camp with the Boy Scouts. Vietnam is a job for a man, and you'd better be a man if you want to go."

"I can handle it."

Cavanaugh nodded with his eyes set hard, still focused on Rick. "Ward, let me tell you something. Politicians think up wars and soldiers fight them. But soldiers in Vietnam don't like the way we're fighting this war. Give us full firepower—nukes or whatever it takes—and we'll kill gooks until the streets run with blood. We'll have this thing over in a few weeks. But that's not what's happening over there. We're fighting a war without the will to win, and now the president is starting to pull us out before we've done the job we went there to do. What I'm telling you is, if you die in Vietnam, it may be for nothing." He sat for a time and let that sink in, and then he added, "So you need to think about your decision."

"I have thought about it." Rick looked down at the table. "I feel like I need what the army can give me."

"What's that?"

Rick couldn't talk about Hemingway or about learning things he could use as a writer, so he told the other truth. "I want to grow up. I want to be a man. I think the army can help me."

Cavanaugh didn't smile, but Rick saw, without question, that the man thought he was an idiot—a kid. It was the look Darrell had given him; the look he had been getting from his dad all his life. But the look steeled Rick's desire. He couldn't stay here. He needed to know the blackest truths the world could show him: hatred, despair, and all the rest. He couldn't write about playing sports in high school or hanging out at the beach. He needed to see what else there was. Vietnam was hell. Maybe so, but Rick was feeling more confident. That's just what he wanted to have a look at.

"The army can help you grow up," the sergeant said, "but most of that will have to come from inside. If I were you, I'd give the whole thing some careful thought. Maybe you'd like to read some of our brochures and—"

"No. I want to sign up. And I want to leave as soon as I can."

"You're eighteen, aren't you?"

"Yes."

"All right. If that's your decision, I'm proud of you. But before you enlist, go home and talk things over with your parents. We'll get your paperwork all set up now, and then you can sleep on it and come back tomorrow if you still want to sign. That's always the best way to go."

So they filled out the papers, and then Rick went home and talked to his mother. She didn't like the idea at all, but when Dad came in, he approved. "That's just exactly what you need, Rick," he said. "You're out of high school and still acting like a baby. The army won't put up with that."

Rick didn't argue. He even told his dad he was sorry about quitting his job, and then Dad said it was all right for him to stick around home until his induction. But Rick wasn't actually sorry that he had quit that stupid job. He mostly just wanted things smoothed over before he left, so his mother wouldn't be too upset. The worst thing was, he still felt like he was running out on her. And no matter what he had said about wanting to be a man, he was scared. He had been since he had walked out of the recruiting office. After he talked to his dad, he went to his bedroom and sat on his bed.

He hated this house. His old iron bed creaked, and the ceiling and one wall were stained yellow from a leak in the roof. He wanted out, but he was also having second thoughts about the army. How could he fight in a war that few people even believed in anymore? But if he didn't enlist, he was right back in his old trap. He lay back and looked at that stained ceiling. He could hear his dad down the hall, his voice a distant rumble. Dad was telling Mom, no doubt, what a smart thing he had done when he had told Rick to get out. It had brought some sense to him. The thought reminded Rick that he was at least sure of one thing: He did have to get out of here.

CHAPTER 3

RICK PASSED HIS PHYSICAL WITHOUT A PROBLEM, AND THEN GOT
word that he'd be heading to Fort Ord in the
Monterey Bay area, three hundred miles north of
Los Angeles on the California coast. He spent the
next two weeks working out every day, running hard
and doing push-ups and chin-ups. Cavanaugh had
said that boot camp would be tough, and Rick
wanted to be ready.

On Rick's last night home, Renny threw a party at
his house, out by the pool. Almost everyone came, all
his old high school friends except Judy. Rick hadn't
talked to her since they'd broken up. Renny had
managed to get some beer and drank too much of it.
Rick had never learned to like beer. He'd seen what it
had done to his dad. It was Renny's business if he
wanted to act like an idiot, but Rick liked knowing he
was in control of himself.

Renny was shooting off his mouth, telling Rick how dumb he was to go into the army. "I don't get this. They're going to ship you straight to Vietnam."

Rick knew better than to respond, but about the fourth time Renny said the same thing, Rick told him, "I don't care if I do go to Vietnam."

There were maybe twenty people at the party, some with dates and some single. Renny and Phil Ford—known mostly as "Flipper"—and another guy, Wayne Rossi, were sitting in deck chairs around a little table by the pool. "Wait a minute. You *want* to go to Vietnam?" Renny said, loud enough for almost everyone to hear.

The girl who had come with Flipper leaned over as if she wanted to look at a freak. Rick stared back. She seemed baffled.

"You heard me," Rick said.

"Why?" Renny demanded. "My brother's waiting to see whether he gets Conscientious Objector status or not. If he doesn't, he's going to Canada. He says he's not going to kill babies for anyone—and certainly not for Dick Nixon."

"There's no way the government's going to get me," Wayne said. "My lottery number is right on the border, but if it comes up, I'm saying, 'Hell no, I won't go.' They can put me in jail if that's what they want to do."

Rick didn't say anything, but he knew there was no way Rossi would have the guts to go to jail. And the whole "killing babies" thing was such a cliché. Renny and Wayne didn't know as much about Vietnam as Rick did. They just knew it was cool to be opposed to the war.

"Come on, man," Renny said. "This is your life! Explain this to me."

Rick tried. "I've been doing the same stuff all my life, Renny. I want to do something else."

It sounded lame. Everyone at the table laughed. Wayne said, "You'll get yourself killed, man. That's the only new experience you'll have over there."

"Come clean, man," Renny said. "Your old man kicked you out of the house and you didn't have a job. Joining the army was the only thing you could think of. That's all."

Rick probably should have left it at that, but he couldn't. Renny was wrong about him. "A guy doesn't know what he's made of until he gets put to the test. You guys are going to hang out here doing nothing, and I'm going to find out what kind of a man I am."

"I know what kind of man I am," Flipper said. "I'm a coward. But that's better than being dead."

"Yeah, Rick," Renny said. "You'll find out you have guts. You'll know when you look down and see them spilling on the ground."

Rick decided not to say anything else, but Flipper's girl asked, "Do you *believe* in the war?"

Rick didn't answer. A couple of guys had grabbed

Jill Rush and were threatening to throw her into the water. She was screaming and giggling and loving every minute of the attention. It was all so superficial, just as Judy had said it was. He had the feeling that twenty years from now Renny and his gang would all be pretty much the same as they were tonight. Well, not him. Rick looked up, gave the girl a long stare—tried, in fact, to look like Sergeant Cavanaugh—and said, "Soldiers don't think up wars. Governments do. I'll do what I'm paid to do, and I'll let the army worry about whether it's right or wrong." The words were all wrong, but he liked the tone he was taking. He wanted to sound independent, gutsy—a man among boys.

"You're going to trust the government?" Renny was asking, but at the same time the girl said, "I personally don't think we have any right to be in Vietnam." It was what every high school kid said these days, but most of them knew hardly anything about the politics of the war. Rick knew some of the history, some of the issues, and the war *was* wrong as far as he was concerned. The Vietnamese had a right to decide for themselves what kind of government they wanted. The United States was actually interfering with that. But Rick wasn't going to admit that, and he wasn't about to say, "I want to find the heart of darkness so I can write like Conrad."

"Rick's not a warrior," Renny said. "He doesn't want to kill anybody. He just wants to get away from his old man. You don't know what he has to put up with."

That was the last thing Rick wanted this crowd to know about. Most of their fathers were professionals. They drove nice cars, dressed well, showed up at ball games when their kids were playing. "Look, Renny," Rick said, "I've got to catch a train early in the morning and I still haven't finished packing. I think I'll—"

"Hey, no. Don't leave like this. We were just giving you a hard time. You're one of us, man—friends forever. You need to get drunk. Come on, I've still got lots of beer left."

"Naw. You know me. I don't like beer." Rick stood up. Jill was out of the pool now. Her long hair hung wet and straight. She wasn't gorgeous, but she looked good. Rick wished he had a girl to say good-bye to. He thought of asking Jill to go for a ride with him. But he would have to talk to her, and he couldn't stand that.

Jill had apparently heard that he was leaving. "Oh, Rick, you're going to wish you'd never joined," she said. "You're too sweet for the army." She touched his arm. She was flirting again. It was probably romantic to her, a soldier going off to war.

"Actually, I'm a born killer," he said. He flexed his biceps and laughed. "Well, I'll see you guys. I'll try to write once in a while."

"How long are you in for?" Flipper asked. He'd taken hold of his girl around the waist.

"It depends. I'm in for two years for sure. But I can put in for Special Forces. If I get in, I'd have to stay an extra year."

"You mean the Green Berets?" Renny asked.

"Yeah."

"You've gotta be kidding. Those guys are insane."

Rick shrugged. He loved the way everyone was looking at him now, especially the girls. "Well, stay loose. I'll look you guys up when I get back from boot camp—if they let me come through here."

"Hey, you gotta say good-bye to everyone," Renny said. "They want to—"

"I sort of did."

Rick left. A few more of his friends stopped him on the way out, but he didn't say much. What was left to say? Nothing would ever be the same. No more of the rah-rah stuff from high school. No more beach parties. Until this instant he'd been telling himself that this was exactly what he wanted to leave behind, but as he got into his car, he felt as though he'd fallen off the planet. In the morning everything he knew would be gone, and he had no idea what to expect from the army.

His Chevy didn't want to start the first time he turned it over. That was all he needed, to run his battery down and have to go back to the party to get someone to give him a jump. He sat and waited for a couple of minutes to make sure he hadn't flooded the carburetor, and this time the engine caught, sputtered, then kicked in. The car had duel pipes, chromed, that put out a gurgling sound. He'd lived for that rumble once, but that time was over now. He'd asked his dad to put the car up for sale and then to bank the money for him.

He knew he ought to head home while his parents were still up. His mom would want to have some time to talk to him. But it was depressing to think about going back there. Besides, there was something else he really wanted to do. It was stupid, but what difference did it make? There was no way to make things any worse. He drove to Judy's house.

When he parked out in front of her place, he almost lost his nerve. But he couldn't bring himself to drive away. He hated the idea of leaving without even saying good-bye. He made himself walk to the door and ring the doorbell. She lived in a nice place, a stretched-out ranch-style house with a Spanish look to it. He'd spent a lot of time there, but he'd almost never taken Judy to his own little house. His dad was too embarrassing, sitting in front of the TV in his thread-bare chair, drinking a beer, thinking he was funny when he tried to tease the two of them.

Judy's mom came to the door. She was wearing shorts and a casual shirt, but as usual her makeup was perfect and her hair was stiff with hairspray. She looked surprised to see Rick. "Oh . . . hello, Ricky," she said.

"Is Judy around?"

"Yes." She hesitated.

"I'm leaving town in the morning. I've joined the army. I just wanted to say good-bye."

"The army?"

"Yes."

He was getting that funny look again, as if she wondered what had possessed him to do something so insane. At least she invited him in. Then she went looking for Judy, who finally appeared in the living room, where he was still standing.

"You joined the army?" Judy said, almost before she had entered the room. She stood with her hands on her hips, an exaggerated look of disbelief on her face. She was wearing jeans that were torn out in the knees. Rick knew she'd bought them not long ago, washed them a dozen times, and torn the holes herself.

"Yeah. I'm heading for Fort Ord in the morning—up by Monterey. But it's a long story. I don't want to get into all that. I just didn't want to leave without at least letting you know."

He saw the stiffness, the disdain, in her face, and he wished he hadn't come. But maybe it was better for him to experience this. If he'd gone off to basic training—or to Vietnam—just thinking of the good days they'd enjoyed together, he would have missed her. Now he would remember this side of her.

"This makes me sick, Rick. You'll end up in Vietnam, and I hate to think what that will do to you."

This was a discussion he didn't want to have. He looked away. "One thing about it, I can use the G. I. Bill to go to college when I get back."

She looked at him as though he'd spoken a foreign language. "Rick, you're a sweet guy. You'll have to make yourself hard as rock. They'll train you to kill. That's the only thing the army knows."

He didn't have an answer for that. Lately he'd tried to imagine himself killing someone. In the movies it was always a great moment when an enemy soldier fell, but he wondered what it might be like to aim at an actual person and pull the trigger. He'd fired a rifle at a shooting range one time—just for target practice—but in truth, he had never killed anything bigger than an insect.

"What about your writing?" Judy asked.

At least he could say something about that. "A lot of writers have gone to war."

"That's what this is about, isn't it? This is your way to get out of here and have some new experiences."

"That's part of it. Most of it, maybe."

She finally walked toward him, but she didn't ask him to sit down. She stood in front of him, still at arm's length, and said, "I can't believe this. Do you really want to fight a war that's morally wrong—just to see what you can learn from it?"

Rick shook his head. "If it's morally wrong, that's not my fault. I'm just going into the army."

"But so many guys are refusing to go! Don't you know what's happening over there?"

He hated the way she was making him feel, so he admitted the truth. "My dad kicked me out of the house. I didn't know what else to do."

Judy studied his face for a long time. Finally she said, "This breaks my heart, Rick. This just isn't you."

But Rick was a little tired of hearing from others about who he supposedly was or wasn't. There was nothing he could say that would change Judy's mind, and nothing he knew strengthened his argument. "Anyway, I just wanted to say good-bye," he said.

"You leave tomorrow?"

"Yeah. So I wanted to tell you thanks for . . . you know . . . everything. I was thinking tonight about some of the things we did together." He looked down at the tile floor. "I guess I'll always be in love with you. Maybe just because you were my first girlfriend."

He couldn't look at her, but he heard her breathe and take a step forward. She touched his arm. "You're so beautiful, Rick. It's the thing I never could resist. You look powerful, but you're soft, really. I don't think many people know that."

"Do you remember that first time we kissed, after my football game?"

"Oh, yes. You were a big hero that night. I can't believe how important football seemed back then."

"I remember the way you looked in that blue sweater you were wearing, with your hair down on your shoulders. I was scared to kiss you, but you made the first move."

Judy laughed. "I was a brazen woman, even then."

"I was thinking about that last night, and I just . . . I don't know." What an idiot he was. "Well, anyway, good luck at Berkeley and everything."

Judy smiled as if she hadn't heard him. "After you kissed me, you held me and held me. I didn't know what it meant. No boy had ever done anything like that with me before."

Rick swallowed and waited a moment before he tried his voice. "I wrote in my notebook last night, if I had to pick the happiest time of my life, that would be it. Standing there with you in my arms that night."

"I was happy too. But we were incredibly young. That was my first *real* kiss, if you know what I mean."

"It was my first . . . whatever you want to call it . . . 'love kiss,' I guess."

Judy nodded. He saw tears in her eyes, but when he tried to take her in his arms, she resisted. She did kiss him briefly, but she held herself away. "Will you write to me?"

"Sure. Do you really want me to?"

"Yes, I really do. We're not right for each other. You know that as well as I do. But that doesn't change how I feel about you. I'll always care for you, and I'll always want to know where you are and what you're doing."

"Okay. I'll write if you'll write back."

"I will." She took hold of his hands. "You're so good, Rick. I hope you won't come back all ugly inside."

Rick didn't like that at all. The next time he saw Judy, he wanted her to see the change in him. He'd be a soldier, a man. She'd have to respect him.

Rick drove home and put up with his dad, who had drunk too much beer and had decided to be "fatherly" this last night. Rick knew what was really making his old man happy. He could release his son to the army and have a few more bucks in his pocket each month.

His mother came to Rick's room while he packed, and she cried. "You were my first little baby," she said. "It never seemed possible that you would grow up so fast. I wish I could hold on to you a little longer. I feel like my heart is leaving with you."

Rick said almost nothing to her. He couldn't. Suddenly he was losing his confidence. When she finally left him alone, he got out his notebook. He had to say what he was really feeling.

44

If I could unenlist from the army, I think I would. I feel like I'm running out on Mom and Roxie. But I have no choice. It's all legal and I signed the papers. Besides, it's what I have to do. If I stayed around here, I'd never change. I'm sick of the things everyone says about me. I may seem soft, but I'm willing to face the enemy and see whether it's him or me.

Rick thought of scratching that out. What did it even mean? But he knew he had a reason to go, even if it was no longer clear to him tonight. So he tried writing again, another way.

I admit I'm scared. I don't know what this war is about. And I don't want to die for no reason. But hardly anyone dies, really. You read about guys getting killed in Vietnam, but when you figure how many go over, it's really a tiny percentage. I probably am too soft, but I'm not going into the army to turn out like one of those bone-brained Marines who run around screaming for blood. It's not like I want to come home all hard and nasty and talking bad. But carrying hod and catching rays on the weekends is like a death sentence to any hope I have of doing something with my life. Maybe I won't be a writer, but at least I need to know that I've been around a little. I talk to guys who were in World War II, and they say, "You don't know until you've been there," and stuff like that. You can tell, they weren't the same guys when they came back. That's all I want. I'm a kid. The hardest thing I've ever done in my life so far is get my weight down for a wrestling match. I've got to do something really important.

I bet Judy finds herself some Berkeley hippie—some guy who writes folk songs and wears sandals. I'm going to write something that will knock her socks off. Someday, she'll tell herself, I could have had Richard Ward, the writer, and I turned him down. I thought I knew him, but I never did. I had no idea what was inside of him.

After Rick put his notebook away, he lay back and thought. Most of what he wrote made sense only about as long as it took to write it. But that didn't matter for now; he'd keep writing. Maybe the day would come when everyone in the country would know his name. He'd write the first great novel about Vietnam maybe—the most honest war book ever written. And he would know it all—the language, the taste of fear, the heightened senses a guy had when death was waiting for him. He'd read some stuff like that, but when he wrote his own novel, he'd be able to nail it all down. He wouldn't be a journalist or a "researcher"; he'd be the real thing: a vet. He felt an uneasiness in his stomach about what he would have to go through to become one, but once he'd been there, he told himself, he wouldn't regret what he'd experienced.

It was getting late and he knew he had to say good-bye to Roxie. She'd still be in bed in the morning when he had to leave. He stepped to her bedroom door and peeked in. "Hey, kid," he said, "I'll see you in a few months, when I get my first leave."

She was sitting on her bed reading a book, as usual. She looked like Mom, with her light hair, round face, round eyes. He and Roxie had talked earlier in the evening, and she'd cried about his leaving. He didn't want to start that again, so he said, "You better not snoop around in my bedroom while I'm gone. It's private property."

"Who'd want to? It smells like dirty socks in there."

He grinned. "I'll leave a few of my old sweat socks around, just so you won't forget me."

She set her book down and got off her bed and hugged him. "Mom's going to cry and cry and cry," she said, with her head against his chest.

"Naw. No way." But he couldn't think of anything else to tell her. He kissed her on the top of her head, held her for a few more seconds, and then patted her shoulder a few times before he left. He shouldn't have glanced back, but he couldn't help it. She was standing in the doorway with tears dripping from her chin. He lay on his bed and tried to think about coming back in triumph. But the image wouldn't come. He could see only dark, as though he were about to walk through a door with nothing on the other side. When the tears finally started, he was sick with himself. He told himself that it was the last time, ever, that he was going to let this happen. But since it *was* the last time, he let go. He rolled over, smashed his face into his pillow, and sobbed.

CHAPTER 4

RICK WAS IN GOOD CONDITION WHEN HE SHOWED UP FOR BASIC training. As it turned out, the physical training was a breeze. A lot of the recruits were in bad shape. Most were smokers and a lot were overweight. For them, the three-mile double-time marches were murder. But the running was nothing compared with what Rick had been used to during two-a-day practices at the beginning of football season or to the hard work he'd put in to get down to weight for wrestling.

The instructional classes during basic weren't very challenging either. The trainers were used to a lot of high school dropouts who could barely read. They explained simple concepts over and over, long after Rick knew the material. Fort Ord itself wasn't much to look at, with its World War II barracks, but the temperatures on the coast were moderate, and the setting along the bay was beautiful. Rick had expected to be tested—pushed to the limit—but so far he was finding everything way too easy.

The time at Ford Ord *was* challenging in one way. Rick had seen movies in which the drill instructors were brutal but idealistic men who pushed recruits hard because they wanted them to be great fighting men. But Rick didn't see much high-mindedness in the sergeants he dealt with. They called the recruits filthy names and harassed them night and day. The name calling was supposed to help the recruits deal with stress in actual combat situations, but it came across to the trainees as just more abuse from a bunch of guys who had gotten themselves a little power after being losers all their lives.

The DIs started in on the recruits the minute they got off the bus, screaming and cursing and humiliating everyone. Rick had been warned; he knew what to expect. But one drill instructor, Sergeant Martin—a thin little guy with gray teeth—had stared Rick in the face and said in his Southern drawl, "You're mine, Beach Boy. They shouldn't let *girls* into this man's army, and you look like a *girl* to me." What followed was an obscene tirade denouncing Rick for his long hair—even though he'd gotten a haircut just before leaving Long Beach—and accusing him of looking like a "homo." Twice Sergeant Martin made Rick drop to the ground to do push-ups and even though Rick touched his chest to the ground every time, the guy kept telling him he wasn't going low enough.

When Rick stood up the second time, Sergeant Martin, with his face just inches from Rick's, screamed at him, "I know what you got inside, sweetheart. Nothing! Nothing at all. You don't have what it takes, recruit. You'll start crying the first time a bullet flies over your head. Ain't that right?"

"No, sir."

"I ain't no sir. What you calling me that for?"

Rick didn't know how to answer.

"I'm a sergeant. You call me Sergeant."

"Yes, Sergeant."

"And I'll call you *Girlie* until you prove to me that's not what you are."

This was a game. Rick knew that, but he didn't see why it was necessary. He had volunteered. He wasn't like these draftees, who had come in angry that they had to serve.

On the following morning Rick's hair was shaved, and then he had to stand in line for his shots. Written tests followed that. Then the running started. Rick went out of his way to show that he wasn't breathing hard after each run. He was clearly in better shape than anyone in his platoon, but Martin didn't back off. He called Rick "Girlie" and "Sweetheart" and "Honeybun"—never called him by his name. He forced Rick to do more push-ups than any of the men, maybe because he could do them so easily.

One day during Rick's third week, he was called out of a training class to report to the headquarters building. He had no idea what it was about, but a staff sergeant named Peterson asked him to sit down. "Ward," he said, from across his desk, "you scored very high on your tests—the highest of any of the new recruits—and Sergeant Martin tells me you're his best man."

"That's interesting, Sergeant," Rick said. "He calls me Girlie."

Sergeant Peterson stared at Rick as if to say, "What else do you expect?" He continued, "When you enlisted, you requested an opportunity to serve with Special Forces. We want you to take another test. If you pass, you could be accepted for Special Forces training after your Advanced Individual Training. Is that something you still want?"

"Possibly, Sergeant." But Rick had begun to have his doubts.

"It means you have to go to jump school first, and you have to sign up for another year—three instead of two."

Rick knew that, and he was no longer sure he wanted to extend his commitment. These first weeks of military life had made two years look long enough. "I don't know, Sergeant. I might want to think about that."

"It's up to you, Ward."

"Sergeant, is it more likely I'll go to Vietnam if I get into Special Forces? I want to get there if I can."

The sergeant looked up from his papers, obviously surprised. He thought for a moment, and then he said, "I'll level with you, Ward. Right now, Special Forces are mostly ending up at Fort Bragg in North Carolina. Not many are going overseas. If you want to get to Nam, the best thing is, take the jump training and get assigned to an Airborne unit. Most of those guys are ending up in the war."

"Is that three years or two, Sergeant?"

"Two."

"That's what I want then, Sergeant. I'd like to be a Green Beret, but not if I'm going to get stuck in the States my whole tour."

"It's up to you."

"I'll take the jump school, Sergeant."

"That's fine. But you'll still have to pass a test. I'll arrange for you to take it."

Rick went back to his class, but he now took a different view of Martin. Maybe Martin actually was trying to get the best out of him. Still, the guy didn't let up. "Where you been, Girlie?" he demanded, and then, before Rick could answer, told him to hit the floor for twenty—because he'd disrupted class.

Boot camp lasted eight weeks. Rick didn't make a lot of friends, but he didn't figure that mattered. Guys would be going off to different Advanced Individual Training programs, and none of these men were likely to end up in jump school with him. Rick had seen guys with Airborne wings. They weren't Green Berets, but they still looked tough— tougher than most of the guys in Rick's training platoon, who seemed more likely to end up as cooks or truck drivers.

Gradually, Rick worked his way into a kind of standoff with Sergeant Martin. The guy still seemed to hate him, but Rick took everything the man handed out—all the insults, all the push-ups—and never flinched, never let Martin know that any of the abuse bothered him. The truth was, he was sick of the whole thing by the time the eight weeks were almost over, but he liked to stare back at Martin with eyes like stone. Sometimes he looked into a mirror as he was shaving, and his face took on that confident, hard-jawed look he remembered from Sergeant Cavanaugh.

Just a few days before basic training was to end, Martin and a couple of other DIs charged into the barracks and shouted that all the men had to fall in for inspection. It was late, just before lights out, and not the usual time for something like this. But shakedown inspections had been common all through the training. From what Rick had heard, the army was worried about drugs getting into the camps and did everything possible to catch men hiding pills or marijuana. At one point the platoon had even been transferred to a different barracks just so the men would be separated from their stashes, if they had any.

Since Rick didn't do drugs, he didn't have a stash to worry about. He always kept his gear squared away, his bunk tightly made, his boots polished. Sometimes Martin had tried to find him making a mistake with the arrangement of his footlocker or wall locker, but Rick had gone out of his way to be sure everything was right all the time. Tonight Martin was going through everyone's gear with special care. When he came to Rick's bunk, he thrust his bony chin close and breathed right into Rick's face. The guy always had bad breath, as though he ate something rank on purpose just before he started these inspections. "What you been smokin', Girlie?" he barked. "You got something stashed in here?" He pointed to Rick's footlocker.

"No, Sergeant," Rick said with confidence.

But Martin didn't look inside. He walked to Rick's bed, grabbed the mattress, and flipped it over. Rick hadn't expected that, and he was suddenly scared. He'd brought his notebook with him and had learned that since it wasn't army issue he couldn't keep it around. He'd thought of sending it home, but he wanted to write down his thoughts from time to time, the way he always had. So he had stuck it in its hiding place. He knew he was taking a chance, but Martin never seemed to check him very closely for drugs, the way he did some of the men. But men had seen him writing, maybe even sticking the notebook back under the mattress. Rick had to wonder now whether someone hadn't ratted him out to Sergeant Martin.

Martin grabbed the notebook as though he'd won a prize. "What's this, Sweet Thing? Dirty pictures of *boys?*"

"No, Sergeant."

Martin opened the notebook and thumbed through it. "So you keep a diary, huh, Girlie? Is that what this is?"

"No, Sergeant."

"Then what is it?"

"I write a few things, Sergeant. That's all." There was a pleading sound in his voice and it embarrassed him, but he felt almost desperate.

"Did you write in here anywhere how much you love me, Sweet Boy? Because I think you got it bad for me—and I don't like that."

"No, Sergeant."

"But you ain't supposed to have something like this."

"No, Sergeant."

Martin was looking more carefully now, turning the pages, stopping to read. Rick was sick. Martin was sure to destroy the book and probably bring him up on Article 15 charges besides. Rick didn't care about the punishment—whatever it was—but he hoped he wouldn't get knocked out of jump school. Even more, he didn't want to lose what he'd written. None of it was very important, but it was a record of the bit of self he had clung to all during these weeks at Fort Ord.

Martin looked down the double row of men who were still at attention at the foot of their bunks. "Men," he shouted, "it looks to me like Girlie has written some nice stories here. Do you want to hear a bedtime story?"

"Yes, Sergeant," the men shouted in unison.

"Well, here's a nice one right here. I want little Sweet Lips to read it to you himself. Nice and loud." He handed the notebook to Rick and pointed to the page.

Rick saw what it was and hesitated.

Martin shouted, "You read that, recruit. Right now. These men want to hear it."

So Rick read a passage he'd written not long after the training had started.

"I don't understand what Sergeant Martin wants from me. I'm in better shape than any of these guys. I could learn this stuff in a tenth of the time, but most of the training is designed for idiots. And we've got plenty of them. It's scary to think of these guys fighting a war for us."

Rick dropped the notebook to his side. He stood at attention, glad that he didn't have to look any of the men in the eye.

"Did you like that story, men?"

"No, Sergeant."

A few had called out yes, obviously unsure what Martin wanted, but Martin said, "Well, now, I don't blame you. That wasn't a very good story. Let's see what else I can find." He grabbed the notebook and began looking through it again. Rick dreaded what might come next.

"Hey, this is good news," Martin finally bellowed. "It sounds like Girlie had him a *girlfriend* and not a boyfriend. I'm surprised by that. Do you men want to hear a nice love story?"

"Yes, Sergeant."

"Read this right here, Girlie."

Rick thought of saying no. Could Martin do this to him? What if he resisted and got himself locked up? Maybe he could show from his record how well he'd done in basic training, and Martin would have to explain himself. But Rick didn't dare take that chance. From what he'd heard, a recruit had no power against the system. He read the passage aloud.

"I miss Judy even though I know she has no feelings for me anymore. Sometimes now, I just want someone like her to talk to. I wrote her the other day, but she hasn't written back. My platoon is full of guys who never say anything worth talking about. Most of them are pretty much brainless. Everybody is always trying to show what *real men* they are. That means being as crude as possible and bragging about how great they are with women. But you can tell they were all a bunch of rejects in high school.

"I wish Judy and I could have kept something going—just to see if anything could have worked out between us. I doubt I'll ever see her again. Boot camp hasn't been very hard physically, but emotionally, it's been tearing me up. I don't fit in anywhere these days. I drifted away from all my friends back home, and I have nothing in common with all these half-wits in my platoon."

The barracks were silent. The men, of course, wouldn't have dared to say anything. Martin would have shut them down immediately. But the silence seemed deep, as though embarrassment were cramming the room. However much they probably hated Rick for what he had written, all these guys must have been wondering what it would be like to have their own private thoughts invaded.

"Did you like that story?" Martin called out.

"No, Sergeant," the men said, but with less volume.

"I didn't either, men. A *man* wouldn't write it. And I wouldn't want to fight alongside a *girl* like this. If I put my life on the line for a soldier, I want to know he's fixin' to do the same for me. A soldier crying about his girl, or talkin' about not 'fitting in'—that's a scared little creep who worries about himself more than the men he fights with." He turned to Rick and said, "This book is mine. And I can tell you right now, you'll be disciplined for having it hidden away like that. I just hope you decide to start acting like a soldier now."

Martin went on with the inspection, and when he was finished he took the notebook with him. After he walked out, a few men called out insults to Rick. But most didn't. And Rick looked at no one. He was thinking that Martin had a point. He didn't blame these guys for hating him. Who was he to act so superior? That's exactly what he had accused Judy of doing.

Rick spent the fall in Georgia, eight weeks at Fort Gordon for Advanced Infantry Training and three weeks at Fort Benning for jump school. By then, he was no longer complaining about not being challenged. The trainees ran long and hard every morning, and fifty push-ups instead of twenty were more likely. Conditions were miserable at Fort Gordon in the coal-heated barracks, and the harassment was intense. The trainers never let up. Every day men dropped out. Paratroopers tucked their trousers into their boots and bloused them. The look set them apart. But after a brutal uphill run or an especially humiliating session with a DI, some men decided they didn't mind settling for a straight-legged unit after all.

Jump school was worse. The inhuman physical training continued, along with the abuse, but the fear of jumping was worse than Rick had imagined. The joke was that jump school separated the men from the fools—the fools jumped. Rick found satisfaction in hanging on, but every night when he fell into his bunk and hadn't washed out of the program, he felt as though steel was replacing his backbone. This is what he had hoped for—and on top of that, when he looked about him, he found men he liked. They weren't necessarily geniuses, but they were as focused and stubborn as he was. One night the black hats burst into the barracks and forced the men to hoist their footlockers over their heads and hold them there. After five minutes, Rick felt close to passing out, but the trainers kept screaming that if *one* guy let his arms down, all the men would get another five minutes. No one broke. After that, Rick looked at the men and knew that he had found what he had hoped for. He was becoming tougher than anyone back home could have believed.

But other times, that wasn't enough. When Rick had left Fort Ord, Sergeant Martin surprised him by returning his notebook and wishing him good luck. The man didn't explain, didn't take back anything he'd said, but just seemed to assume that Rick understood what had been going on. Rick had sent the notebook home in a package marked DO NOT OPEN, so he hadn't been able to write since then. Sometimes, as he was falling asleep, or during brief breaks, he wondered what he'd have written if he'd kept the book with him. He was startled by how little came to mind. He'd found it interesting to meet men from all around the country, but he'd also found that most of them were just guys. Young guys. The biggest difference between them and his friends was that most of them were volunteers, not draftees, and they said they wanted to get to Nam. Renny, of course—and almost all the guys in basic training—had thought that was stupid.

Rick wanted to feel something new. Maybe that would come with war, but he wasn't certain any longer. He did what he had to do each day, and yet inside he was still just the same. He couldn't really say that he was closer to calling himself a man. He'd made it through the training, but he'd also hated every second of it. He'd learned the skill of killing, had practiced all the techniques, but he hadn't learned why he had to do it. He had screamed about hating gooks, but he *didn't* hate them, and he *did* hate that word.

He had heard an amazing amount of propaganda from his trainers. They insisted that the war was all about saving the world from Communism. American soldiers had to fight harder than ever, they said, so the battle could be turned over to South Vietnamese troops. College students and protesters didn't know the truth and were traitors to America.

Rick said the things he was supposed to say, but he only believed a little of it. He wondered whether other men were doing the same. One jump school trainee, a guy named Max Lender, told Rick that Nixon was a liar and Lyndon Johnson had been even worse. He didn't believe any of the garbage they were being fed. When Rick asked him what he was doing there then, Max said, "I don't know. My dad was in World War II and my brother's in Nam. I've heard all their stories."

It seemed a strange answer, but when Max asked Rick why he had joined up, Rick could only think to say, "I didn't have the money to start college." He had the feeling that most of the guys around him didn't have any better reasons. Whether they admitted it or not, they were tired of their lives. Vietnam was their chance to see what war was all about.

By the time Rick went home for his two-week leave, he felt empty. He saw Renny once, but he decided he didn't want to see him again. He didn't know what to say to the guy. He hadn't heard a word from Judy, and she was away at school now. Mostly he felt nervous. He was actually more frightened than when he had first left home, but he didn't know what he feared—maybe that none of what he'd experienced meant anything. He'd spent almost six months in the army, and the training was supposed to make him eager and able to fight. But he was about to fight an enemy he didn't hate, for a cause that no one could intelligently justify.

So Rick was going to Vietnam. It was what he had to do next. He'd made a decision just out of high school. It seemed like a decade had passed since then. But there was no going back.

CHAPTER 5

WHEN RICK STEPPED OFF THE AIRPLANE AT TON SON NHUT AIRFIELD in Vietnam, he felt a wave of heat that was unlike anything he'd ever experienced. It was a wall of steam so thick he thought he could put out his hands and lean on it. He'd thought Georgia was humid, but this air was too heavy to breathe. And the stench was even worse. A soldier who had done a previous hitch in Nam had told Rick that the smell was from burning sewage. There was no way to get rid of human waste, so the troops poured gasoline onto it and ignited it. The foul smoke drifted everywhere. The smell was pretty much the same at most of the bases.

Rick and the others from his airplane were herded onto olive drab buses with barred windows and transported to the 90th Replacement Battalion, the "repo depot." Rick's bus passed through a ramshackle town called Bien Hoa. Cars, bicycles, and motorcycles, along with big army deuce-and-a-half trucks filled the narrow streets, but there seemed to be no rules, no order to the traffic. The people lived mostly in hooches made of cardboard and corrugated metal, some of them up on stilts. Half the businesses were little bars or brothels. Most of the people in the streets were dressed in loose black pajamas and conical-shaped hats. The kids were more or less naked.

The sergeant who processed Rick's paperwork at the base was way too much like the smell and the heat: alien and hostile. He seemed to hate Rick for no reason that Rick could imagine, and nothing annoyed the man more than questions. "You'll find out," was all he would say. "No one can tell you new guys anything right now. Just remember, you're not in the world anymore." "The world" was the term that soldiers used for America—for life back home—no part of which resembled Vietnam.

It took two days of bad food, restless sleep in the heat, and a few worthless work assignments before Rick got his assignment to the 173rd Airborne Brigade, camped near Bien Hoa. But first Rick and a lot of his friends were being shipped to the Cha Rang Valley, where they would receive jungle training. As they flew, Rick looked down on a country so green it hardly seemed real—a kind of paradise. But when he boarded a bus again, he saw that everything was covered with red dust, and the people on the street stared at

Americans with hatred in their eyes, sometimes even yelling obscene insults in English. It was disturbing. Weren't these the people he had come to save from the Communists? They obviously didn't believe it any more than he did.

Rick's jungle training started with an orientation meeting in a big, smelly tent. He liked the look of the Airborne men in their jump boots and camouflage fatigues, and he learned a lot, quickly, about strategies in the jungle. But he was most impressed when a muscular sergeant named Carver stood up and said, "I'm looking for a few select men who would like to fight alongside the best soldiers over here." He paused and looked around. "I'm talking about the Charlie Company Rangers. We're a special unit. We go out on long-range patrols. You may have heard about L-R-R-P units—what we usually call 'Lurps.' That's long-range reconnaissance patrol. That's all well and good. But we're different. They still call us Lurps sometimes, but we're not a reconnaissance unit. We insert into the jungle in six-man teams. We hunt down the enemy and kill him. We move in silence and we beat the North Vietnamese at their own game. We take on dangerous duty, but we come back alive because we're good at what we do." He waited and let all that sink in. "This is not something most of you will want to do. You're in a fine outfit right now. But if you think you have the capacity to push yourself to another level—elevate what you expect of yourself one more notch—just raise your hand. We'll talk to you and then decide if we want to give you a try."

No hands went up. Rick was still thinking. This duty sounded like the thing he had been looking for from the beginning. Sergeant Carver waited for a time and then seemed ready to turn and leave. Suddenly Rick's hand shot up, almost before he'd made his decision.

"Okay, soldier," Carver said. "Step outside with me."

What followed was a short interview. Carver was clearly pleased. "You have the qualities we're looking for," he told Rick. "Just say the word and I'll get your orders cut. We'll send you to Ranger school when you finish here. If you do all right there, we'll bring you in to Charlie Company, but if you show any sign that you aren't fit to go out with us, we'll ship you back here immediately. We can't afford *any* weak links."

Rick had wanted Special Forces, and this was similar. Rangers were known for being hard core, and he wouldn't have to extend his tour. Still, he had doubts. "No matter what you say about coming back alive, this duty sounds more dangerous than what I'll be doing with the 173rd."

"That's where you're wrong. These Airborne guys are all right, but they tromp through the jungle like a herd of elephants. The gooks hear them from miles away, hide and wait, then pick away at them. These guys are taking casualties every time out, and no one I know humps the jungles more than they do. When Charlie Rangers go out, we're in the boonies three or four days. We kill with precision. Then we get out. When it's done right, no one gets hurt—no one but a lot of gooks."

Rick didn't really like the big talk. But the guy had eyes like ice cubes. Rick had already seen too many soldiers with peace signs on their helmets. If he was going to be a soldier, he might as well be with men who got it right. "All right, sign me up," he said.

By the time Rick completed his jungle training, his orders had come through. He spent two weeks at An Khe in Ranger training. The men ran hard and often, and they had to learn every specialty that the six-man teams needed so they could cover for each other if a soldier went down. Rick received training in radio operation, first aid, map reading, night navigation, advanced weapons, and ambush techniques, and he learned to rappel and to make quick jungle insertions and extractions from helicopters. At the end of the two weeks, he felt as prepared as he'd ever be, short of experiencing the real thing.

He was flown on a Huey helicopter to a camp near Phan Thiet, a little fishing village on the South China Sea. Charlie Rangers were not tied to any one unit. They had a major for a commanding officer, not a captain, and they moved from time to time according to where they were needed, but they were likely to stay around Phan Thiet for a while.

Rick checked in at the Tactical Operations Center, which was just one more green tent in a whole city of tents. The area was bleak, with no trees and little grass. A sergeant processed Rick's papers and then sent him down a sandy red road to his quarters—a huge tent, big enough for a platoon. The side flaps were rolled up so air could get through, but no air was moving, and the stacks of sandbags around the outside would have blocked a breeze anyway. The smell wasn't as bad here, but Rick could smell himself. He was soaked through just from the effort of carrying his duffel bag this far. No one was around, so Rick started squaring away his gear, as he'd been trained to do. After a couple of minutes someone walked into the tent. "Are you the FNG?"

Rick swung around, wondering whether he needed to salute. But the soldier was a corporal, and young— maybe nineteen or so. "The what?" he asked.

"The new guy."

"Oh. Yeah, I am."

The corporal wasn't smiling, and he didn't reach to shake hands. Rick wasn't exactly sure how men did things out here, but he certainly wanted to make friends with the soldiers in his platoon. "Did they tell you to take that bunk?" the corporal asked.

"No," Rick said. "But the sergeant up at TOC told

me to find an empty one, and this was the only one I could see. Is it okay?"

The corporal cursed for no apparent reason and said, "Sure. What do I care?"

Rick hesitated, unsure how to respond, but he finally stuck out his hand. "My name's Rick Ward," he said.

"John Duffy," the soldier said. "But don't call me that. I'm J. D." He gave Rick a brief handshake. He was a thin guy with a bony face marked with lots of acne scars. He was a lot shorter than Rick, and his camouflage fatigues—what the men called "jungle utilities"— had lost most of their color from wear. The truth was, he didn't look like one of the crack soldiers that Rick had been hearing about.

"They tell me Charlie Rangers are the best," Rick said, mostly just to say something.

"You ain't no Charlie Ranger yet," J. D. said. "So don't start acting like you're some steely eyed killer." Then he cursed again.

"Hey, I know. I'm here to learn."

"You're fresh meat. That's what you're here for." J. D. turned and walked out.

Rick had no idea what J. D was talking about, but he was unnerved. He continued to put his equipment away, but he was wondering what he'd gotten himself into. The sergeant who had sent him to the tent hadn't said what Rick should do once he'd set himself up, so Rick took his time. Then, once he had finished, he simply sat on his bunk. He thought about writing in his notebook, which he'd brought with him from home, but he was too nervous. He wondered where his platoon was. Maybe they were in the jungle and he'd have some days to wait. It would be just like the army not to bother to tell him. But Rick hoped that wasn't true. He didn't want time to think. He needed to get out on his first mission and get some mud on his boots so he looked like the other men.

Finally another man entered the tent. He was tall and well built and he looked older than most guys Rick had seen, but he was only a PFC—private first class. He looked so friendly that Rick's first thought was that he must be a cook or something, not a fighting man.

"You must be Ward," he said. "My name's Kent Richards." He put out his hand.

Rick stood up and shook it. "Yeah. Rick Ward. Who told you my name?"

"I talked to Sergeant Bickers, over at the TOC. He told me you got in."

"Do you bunk here too, or . . ."

"Yup. Right there next to you, actually. You're assigned to our team. And I'm glad you got here. That means *you're* the new guy and I'm not."

Rick suddenly realized why new guys were called FNGs. He didn't have to ask what the F stood for. "What do the men have against new guys?" he asked.

Richards smiled. He reminded Rick of a Sunday School teacher he'd had when he was a kid—a good guy, but maybe a little too nice for Rick's taste. Richards walked past Rick and sat on his cot. "I'm still not sure what it's all about, but I have a theory."

"What's your theory?"

"They don't actually hate you. That's the main thing to remember."

Rick wanted to sit down, but there wasn't much room if he sat facing Richards, so he remained standing. "That's not the impression I got from J. D.," he said.

"Was he in here?"

"Yeah. But not for long."

Richards nodded. He looked serious for the first time. "The soldier who used to have this bunk was a good friend of his. He got hit with AK-47 fire last week. He's alive, but he's in bad shape. They shipped him to a hospital in the States."

Rick wasn't quite sure he got the point. "So J. D. is down about that?"

"Well, yeah. And then you came in and took his bunk."

"What else can I do? Is there somewhere else I can go?"

"No. That's not the point. But you came in for him. I don't think I can explain it."

"Give it a try." The whole thing angered Rick. J. D. was hostile for no reason. And Richards was annoyingly polite. Rick hoped the rest of the men in the platoon weren't anything like these guys.

"The men who've been around for a while figure that new guys are dangerous. They're the ones who are most likely to mess up and get a team in trouble. But there's another part of it, I think. After you get to be friends with a guy and he goes down, you don't want to get too close to the next one who comes in. You don't want to go through something like that again. And new guys get killed a lot faster than anyone else."

Rick felt some air go out of him. It was obvious, no matter what Carver had said, that guys did get shot up in this company. And some of them died.

"You have to earn their respect, but that's all right," Richards said. "That's how it has to be."

Rick was suddenly unsure that he was ready for this six-man hunt-and-kill stuff. He'd never thought about what would happen if he made a mistake. It was eerie, too, taking over the cot of a man who had gotten himself shot up.

"Where are you from?" Richards asked.

"Long Beach. Southern Cal," Rick said.

"And you go by Rick—not Richard?"

"Right."

"You'll probably end up with another nickname. Almost everyone does. They call me Preacher. But don't call me that. Just call me Kent."

"Why do they call you Preacher?" It felt awkward

standing above Richards, so Rick sat down on his cot and then turned as best he could. The humid heat in the tent was intense. What was it going to be like to sleep in here?

"I was a Mormon missionary in Uruguay for two years." Richards laughed. "I didn't advertise that when I came in, but everyone found out."

"How'd you end up over here if you're a missionary?"

"I'm not a minister. A lot of people in our church serve missions for two years. After my mission, I finished college at Utah State, but I got drafted as soon as I graduated."

"So you're from Utah?"

"Southern Idaho, just across the border from Utah. A little town called Franklin."

This guy was even older than Rick had thought. He had to be at least twenty-five. "Why didn't you put in for officer's school if you're already out of college?"

"I'd have to stay in longer. I wanted to be finished in two years."

Rick nodded. That he did understand. "I knew some Mormons in my high school. They all had big families."

"Some do. I've only got a brother and two little sisters."

"*Only* four of you, huh?"

"Well, yeah. But there are some *big* families in the town where I live."

"You must be really religious."

Richards smiled. He had a wide mouth that stretched even more when he smiled, and it made him look like a kid. His hair was tousled and blond, longer than Rick was used to, but everything seemed a little less by-the-book here. "Sure I am. What about you?"

"I don't know. My mom used to take me to church when I was a kid, but I haven't gone for quite a while. I don't really give that kind of stuff much thought."

"A lot of guys don't." Kent grinned again. "But most of them get religion when a firefight starts."

"So is it pretty rough—these long-range patrols?"

"It's no walk in the park, I can tell you that. You'll see what's going on soon."

"Did I—you know—do the right thing, volunteering for something like this?"

Kent looked at the reddish sand floor. "I'll let you decide. But if you go out on your first patrol and don't like it, just say the word and they'll ship you back to a line unit."

"Which is more dangerous—this or the 173rd Airborne?"

"That's exactly the same question I asked myself when I listened to Carver's sales pitch. 'You'll come back alive,' he told us, and I bought it."

"Isn't it true?"

"We know what we're doing. We strike fast and get out. That helps. On the other hand, we go out looking for trouble and we find it—plenty of it. We've lost quite a few of our men."

"What about the 173rd?"

"They go out and stay out. I did that with them for a while. They're in the jungle most of the time, in all the heat, with snakes and bugs and leeches. Lousy food. And there's so many of them, they can't keep quiet. I spent about a month with the 173rd, and now I've been here almost two. I don't know who has the higher casualty rate, but I feel safer with these guys. Too many guys in regular units are out there in the field smoking dope. These guys may do that a little around camp, but in the jungle, they don't mess around, ever." Kent laughed. "Of course, all in all, I'd rather be shuffling papers in some office back in the rear."

"I thought men at the front hated those guys."

"They do. But I don't know many who wouldn't trade, at least if they were being honest." Kent hesitated and then added, "Except some of these Rangers are pretty scary. It's like they have a taste for blood and they always want more. I try to act the way a Christian should—you know, think the best of these guys—but some of them are hard to take, and they can't stand me. I get sick of all this preacher talk, and all the knocks on my religion."

"They make cracks about that?"

"Oh, yeah." Kent was smiling now. "And I'll tell you something. One of these times I'm going to show

77

somebody how I used to wrestle steers, back in my rodeo days. These guys think they're bad, but they're mostly talk. I could handle any of them."

"Are you serious?"

"Yeah, I am." Kent looked down. "I shouldn't be. I know that. But I get fed up with these guys sometimes."

Rick adjusted his opinion of Kent a little. But his mind was mostly elsewhere. He could deal with the jerks, he figured, but he wasn't sure about the rest. He wondered how he would react when he finally got himself into a firefight. And something else was bothering him. "Is all of this worth it?"

"What do you mean?"

"Are we actually doing any good over here?"

Kent stared at him for a time, as though Rick's question didn't quite make sense. "What do you mean? Do you think we're *winning* the war?" he finally asked.

"Not winning. But aren't we supposed to be getting ready to turn the fight over to the South Vietnamese? That's all we heard about back in the States."

Kent looked baffled. "Listen, Rick," he said, "we just do what we have to do. No one talks about how the war will turn out. We go out on patrols and look for people to kill. We kill them if we can. Then we count the bodies. It's called 'search and destroy.' We don't take land and hold it. We don't advance a front. We just try to kill them until they stop coming—but they don't stop coming. They never will. We kill lots more of them than they kill of us, but it doesn't matter. The North doesn't run out of people to send, and a lot of the ones they do send are just young boys. From what I hear, they have a never-ending supply. They've been fighting us and fighting the French for generations, and they'll never quit."

"I know all that. But I figured the guys who fought here—at least the Rangers—must believe in what they're doing."

"I don't know. Maybe some do. But it's not anything we talk about. I think in the early years a lot of guys thought we were winning and stopping Communism and all that, but since the Tet Offensive last year—and all the withdrawal plans—men just worry about the problem right in front of them. Staying alive."

"So how do you keep yourself going?" That question had been on Rick's mind a great deal lately. He'd been curious to see what war was, but he hadn't thought enough about the actual act of going to war day after day. What he had been wishing since he arrived in country was that he had a better reason for being here.

"My government drafted me, and I'm loyal to my country. But what we talk about is getting our three hundred sixty-five days in and going home. Every man here knows how many days he has left. Me, I've got two hundred seventy-four, which is the same as forever. Some of the guys in our platoon are pretty crazy—you know, really *into* what we do out in the jungle. But I've never heard any of them say anything about winning the war. Or even anything about the ARVN winning, after we pull out. Everyone knows the South Vietnamese have no chance against the North."

Rick felt as though he'd wandered into a bad dream. The war made no sense to him, but he'd assumed the soldiers found their reasons for believing in what they did. Back in training there had been plenty of talk about fighting for what was right. It was unnerving to hear that soldiers on the front were thinking only about getting their year in, then going home. And worse to think how long a year would be in this place.

"What I wish is that no one had ever thought up this whole mess," Kent said. "I keep thinking that God must weep when He sees what's going on in Vietnam."

Rick tried to think about that, but he couldn't concentrate. He wondered whether he would ever be able to take a long, relaxing breath again.

CHAPTER 6

BEFORE THE DAY WAS OVER, RICK MET THE OTHER MEN IN HIS
platoon. Most of them were returning that day from
jungle patrols. They were dirty and smelled bad, and
they were glad to get a shower and some sleep. The
men from one team came in talking louder than the
others, bragging about the kills they'd gotten. Rick
didn't hear the whole story, but they'd apparently set
up an ambush and killed three North Vietnamese
soldiers with claymore mines and rifle fire. Rick
heard the team leader, a crusty-looking staff sergeant
with burly arms and legs, say, "You should have seen
it, man. These three gooks came through, just half-
stepping. When the claymores went off, two of 'em
bought it right there. Blood and brains flew all over
the place. The other little guy tried to run and we cut
him down. Jimmy put a new zipper up his back—hit
him about six times."

Rick hardly knew what to make of that. He'd worried sometimes about killing, but the sergeant was laughing, and the other men obviously liked the story. Maybe it wasn't such a hard thing to do, once you got used to it.

Rick's team, second platoon, fourth team—called the "two-four"—had been held in reserve while the other teams had gone into the field. Rick found out that one team was always held out in case one of the others got in trouble and needed help. The casualty his team had recently taken had put them on that reserve status this time around. Rick's team leader was a staff sergeant named Zeller. He was small and tightly built. He told Rick, "Talk to Whiley and J. D. about the gear you need to carry when you go out the first time. You'll be packing the thump gun, and that's heavy, so I hope you're in good shape."

"That won't be a problem, Sergeant," Rick assured him, but the look in Zeller's hard eyes made Rick nervous. Zeller didn't seem the sort of guy who would accept mistakes.

Whiley Green turned out to be a big, powerful Texan who, at twenty, was starting to lose his hair. He was loud and foulmouthed, and he started in on Rick immediately. He knew several crude names for "new guy," and he used them all. He wasn't as hostile as J. D.—his abuse seemed mostly in fun—but he warned Rick: "We're going to teach you a lot in the next few days. Stuff you didn't learn in training. You listen to every word, and you get it right. I'm not going to let you get us all killed."

A buck sergeant named Sparks, a black guy who looked more like a university student than a soldier, was the ATL—assistant team leader. He was more relaxed and friendlier than most of the men, but Kent said he was all business in the jungle. "Don't let Whiley and J. D. bother you," Sparks told Rick. "They have mouths on 'em, but they get it right when they're out in the woods."

"Out in the woods." That was the phrase the men used, and even the way they said it made the patrols sound spooky.

But the men in the two-four worked with him. They taught him what to carry, how to tape his strap clips so they wouldn't rattle, what to pack in the ruck-sack. He would be carrying fifty pounds on his back: dehydrated "Lurp rations" for meals, canteens, and a poncho liner for bedding. Strapped on top of the ruck-sack would be the M79 grenade launcher—the thump gun—and he'd have grenades attached to his web gear around his waist, twenty M-16 ammo magazines in his pockets, and an M-16 rifle in his hands. He'd practiced insertions and silent movement in heavy brush, but he'd never done it carrying that much weight. He wondered whether he could even jump from the Huey transport helicopter—called a "slick" by the men—and stay on his feet.

When he walked to the helipad at 0530 for his first long-range patrol, he was feeling the weight of more than the rucksack and his gear. His hands were shaking and he had cotton mouth. But Zeller pulled him aside, out there in the dark, with the sun not yet rising. "We'll take care of you, Ward," he said. "Watch and listen. You don't have to make a lot of decisions. Just remember what you've been taught and follow what we do."

"I'm fine, Sergeant."

"No, you're not. You're scared to death. But that's not all bad. Fear keeps a man sharp."

Sparks would be the point man on this mission, and Kent would be in "slack" position, following Sparks. Zeller would walk third, where he could run the show from the middle, and J. D. was his radio man, behind him. Rick was walking fifth, and Whiley would handle rear security.

Rick heard a distant hum, then listened as the rhythmic sound of the chopper blades became more distinct. When the slick touched down, the men bent over and ran under the blades, then jumped on as assigned. Rick was on the left side, next to Whiley, both of them sitting with their legs hanging outside. Sparks and Kent rode the same way on the right. Zeller and J. D. sat on the steel floor in the middle. The engine wound tight, whining much more loudly than Rick had expected, and then the slick lifted off and nosed away. Rick watched the horizon, where the sun was beginning to light the sky. The South China Sea was still black below them. The Huey swung to the west and rushed hard over a wide plain and then, as it reached the jungle, over dark, thick vegetation. Rick had done as he'd been taught that morning: applied insect repellent on his hands and face, then applied camouflage over that in black and green splotches. What he hadn't known was that the stuff would make his face itch when he started to sweat, and he was sweating already, even with the rush of air around him.

They hadn't been flying long, maybe fifteen or twenty minutes, when Zeller barked, "Lock and load." Rick already had a magazine in his hand, but it took him a couple of tries to push it into his M-16 with his shaking hands. He jacked the charging handle and chambered a round. The door gunner, part of the helicopter crew, was locking in a belt of ammo at the same time, readying his M-60 machine gun.

Rick felt the Huey dive and a wave of nausea passed through his gut, but then the nose of the slick flared up and the pilot brought them down into a little open patch in the jungle. There was more light now, and Rick watched the elephant grass flatten as the slick hovered close to the ground. Before the skids touched down, Whiley jumped to the ground. Rick dropped behind him, stumbled under the weight he was carrying, but caught his balance and ran hard behind Whiley to the vegetation under the canopy of the jungle. All six men gathered in a tight perimeter, thirty or forty feet beyond the tree line, then got down and waited. No one moved, and once the sound of the slick disappeared, everything was silent. This was the dangerous time. If the team had inserted too close to the enemy, the men could be overrun in a matter of minutes.

They waited and listened. Fifteen minutes. Rick's heart was pounding so loudly in his ears, he could hardly tell what was happening in the jungle around him, but he kept glancing toward Whiley on his left and Kent on his right, and they seemed unconcerned. They were obviously hearing nothing that worried them. It was a cold insertion. The mission would continue.

J. D. did a communications check with X-ray, the team that relayed radio contact to the TOC back at the camp. "I've got you the same, Lima Charlie," J. D. whispered, code words for "loud and clear." Two other teams were inserting that morning, all in the same general Area of Operation. Each would work on its own, but if things got hot for one team, another could sometimes move in and join forces.

Finally Zeller clicked his fingers softly to get the men's attention, and then he used a hand signal to wave them forward. They all got up, carefully, silently, and Sparks moved out ahead. Rick had done all this in training, but now the progress seemed painfully slow. The men took one step at a time, picking up their feet and placing them carefully, avoiding all sound. If a thorny wait-a-minute vine or a limb caught hold of a rifle or a man's arm, he had to place it back where it had been, not allow it to flip back on its own. No one spoke. A cough had to be muffled in the crook of a man's arm, and if a mosquito landed on his face, there was no slapping, no quick movement.

It was tedious work, but the men gradually made their way down the hillside. There was a wide high-speed trail at the bottom of this valley. It ran alongside a creek—called a "blue line" because creeks and rivers were drawn in blue on maps. The plan was to set up an ambush along the trail and then wait. There had been enemy movement spotted in this part of the jungle, and Zeller's team was going to set up claymores that could blast thousands of steel pellets across the trail. If the men could find the right sort of ambush site, they would line up a whole series of mines, wire them together with detonator cord in a daisy chain, then watch for enemy troops to enter the kill zone. With one motion of a clacker, the mines would all go up. Rick had seen what the claymores could do to vegetation; he could only imagine what they would do to a soldier in the kill zone. The trick for the team was to find a place to observe enemy movement without getting so close to the mines that their own men would be caught in the vicious back blast.

For the moment, though, Rick wasn't worried about any of that. He was still taking cautious steps and keeping his proper interval behind J. D. The barrel of the thump gun continually caught in the vines, and it was all he could do to keep up. Whiley helped him a few times, but Whiley was usually walking backward, watching behind and sanitizing the trail by lifting flattened vegetation so it wouldn't look as if they'd walked on it.

The movement was not only laborious but exhausting, and the temperature was rising. Rick's camo fatigues were soaked through, and even with his boonie hat on, sweat kept running into his eyes. He had learned from the others to carry a towel around his neck and to pat the sweat on his face without wiping the camouflage away. Twice Zeller snapped his fingers and then waved the men into cover where they could rest. Rick was carrying a lot of water, which was heavy, but he was glad he had it. Zeller had told him to drink the water freely or risk heat exhaustion. They would reach the stream that day, and that would give them a chance to refill their canteens.

On the second stop, the men opened a Lurp meal— all dehydrated—added water, then ate quickly, one at a time, while the others stayed on watch. They buried the foil wrappers, covered the hole so it couldn't be detected, and moved on.

It was afternoon when the men reached the trail they were looking for. Zeller whispered with Sparks for a time, and then he waved the men together. "I don't like walking a trail," he said, "but we'll have to do it. It'll take us too long to walk parallel in this brush. We'll try to find an ambush site close by." Rick didn't know how much longer he could keep going. At least the trail would be easier to walk. But he also knew what Zeller meant. Trails were dangerous. The North Vietnamese Army liked to set up ambushes, the same as Charlie Rangers did. It was a chancy way to travel if enemy troops were in the area, especially if they had heard the insertion that morning.

The men moved out again, Sparks watching the trail for booby traps, still walking slowly. The slow-motion steps were strenuous beyond belief, but Rick was glad for the care Sparks was taking, and he was amazed at the discipline around him. Whiley and J. D. had seemed like loose guys back at the base, but they were silent here, and they moved like hunting cats, just like everyone else. It was consoling to see such precision around him, but Rick wondered now who might be out there under the triple canopy of the jungle. A sniper could be in any of the high teak trees, and he could have his sights on Rick. The chatter of monkeys, of birds, the buzz of insects—any sound—

startled him, again and again. The odor of rotten jungle vegetation was strong, but Rick could still smell his own sweat. All the men said that NVA soldiers could pick up the smell of Americans from a long distance. "We can smell them, too," J. D. had assured Rick. "Gooks smell a lot worse than us from eating fish heads and stuff like that, and most of the time, they don't know we're around." Rick wanted to believe that, but he'd had no idea that the quiet, the half-light, the thick air, would all feel so alien and evil.

An hour passed, and several times Zeller and Sparks conferred, but no ambush site satisfied them, so they kept moving, watching for the right spot. Rick didn't know enough to pick the site, but he watched the jungle on both sides, moving his eyes, not his head, as he'd been taught at Ranger school. He was glancing down, watching where he was placing his foot, feeling good that he was doing all right, when an explosion of gunfire cracked the silence. He was paralyzed for a moment, unsure what had happened. Then he saw a flash, heard the intense zipping sound as Sparks fired his weapon. Tracers were flying back at Sparks, and the sound of automatic fire was blasting from the jungle. Rick dove off the trail and rolled into a thick growth of ferns. He grabbed his helmet, curled up, and held on. There was another rattling blast, then another, and then he heard Kent say, "Sparks is down."

But already there was rifle fire again, and Rick

didn't know what was happening. He heard men moving, then more automatic fire from the jungle. Rick knew he had to get up. He had to fight with his team. He rolled out of his cover and got onto his feet, but he stayed hunched. Everyone had moved up the trail and Zeller was in front now, shooting. Rick knew he had to help, but he couldn't get himself to take a step. Then he saw movement above the trail in the brush, off to his right. He was suddenly firing his M-16 wildly, not aiming, just spreading bullets into the cover. He heard bullets around him, saw tracers, but he didn't drop down again. He kept firing, trying to see, wanting desperately to destroy whatever was out there.

Then everything stopped. His ammo magazine was empty. He ejected it and reached into his pocket for another one. By then Zeller was calling, "We gotta get Sparks to a landing zone. J. D., call in Cobras and a dustoff."

But Whiley was saying, "It's too late. Sparks is wasted."

Rick couldn't believe it. He saw Zeller on one knee, next to Sparks, who was lying on the trail. When Zeller rolled Sparks onto his back, the man's face was nothing but blood and ripped-up flesh.

"We still need gunships and a slick," Zeller said. "Tell 'em we'll get to an LZ. There's a place back down the trail where they can get in. We'll pop smoke so they can find it."

Zeller and Kent each grabbed Sparks by one arm, and they walked hard toward Rick, dragging the body. Rick moved out of the way. He wanted to help, but he didn't know what to do. "Come on," Zeller told him. "Those NVA dropped back, but they'll be on us again."

So Rick followed behind Zeller and Kent as they pulled Sparks. Rick could see a hole in Sparks's gut, could even see his insides bulging through the skin. His body had been ripped straight up the middle. There was another hole in his chest, and his jaw was almost torn off. Rick kept turning to watch the trail, but J. D. and Whiley were covering the team, taking turns running, then stopping and spinning around, rifles at the ready.

The team charged ahead maybe a hundred and fifty meters, and then Zeller said, "Ward, help Preacher with Sparks." Zeller ran ahead and then broke off and sloshed through the little stream alongside the trail. When Rick and Kent followed, Zeller called for them to cross over, so they pulled Sparks through the stream and broke into a little clearing on the other side. "Find some cover," Zeller told them.

J. D. caught up just then. "We got gunships three mikes out," he said, "and a slick right behind them."

A mike was a minute. Rick thought three minutes sounded good, but as seconds slowly passed, he began to think it was a long time.

The men spread out around the landing zone and

watched for movement. Whiley stayed at the stream and kept his eye on the trail.

Rick was sure three minutes must have passed when J. D. called, "Okay. One mike. Get ready with the smoke."

Zeller waited until the sound of the rotors was fairly loud, and then he tossed a smoke grenade into the center of the clearing. Purple smoke began to billow into the air.

In a few more seconds J. D. said, "They've got our smoke. They confirmed the color."

"Tell those Snake pilots to rake the blue line, from our smoke up the valley," Zeller told him.

By then Rick could see two thin black Cobra gunship helicopters angling toward them, dropping fast. As they passed over the smoke, the door gunners opened up with automatic fire, tearing up the jungle along the stream. It was unbelievable, the noise and the power, the dust. The whole valley seemed to be blowing up. And now the slick was diving toward the LZ. Rick and Kent grabbed Sparks and ran under the rotors. Zeller ran past them and jumped on first, then helped pull Sparks on, and everyone clambered in behind him. While Whiley was still standing on a skid, the slick pulled up, then dropped its nose and skimmed away over the trees. And suddenly Rick knew he was all right.

But there was Sparks on the floor next to him,

blood still spilling from his open abdomen, his face torn open, his skin gray. Rick turned his head. He couldn't look anymore.

Whiley grabbed Rick's arm and yelled into his ear, "Don't look away, new boy. Take a good, long look at him."

Rick ignored Whiley and tried to twist away. He wanted to get closer to the door. He needed air.

But Whiley had hold of Rick's arm in a painful grip. He pulled Rick back around and shouted, "How do you like war so far, Ward? Just like in the movies, ain't it? Lots of fun."

Rick took another look at the body, but he didn't look at the shredded face. Sparks was from Baltimore. He was a big Orioles fan. That was almost the only thing Rick knew about him. And now he'd been turned into a bloody lump. Rick really needed to vomit, but he kept swallowing hard, and then, as Whiley loosened his grip, he leaned toward the rush of air from the door. That helped a little, but he was thinking he couldn't keep doing this over and over. Not for a whole year.

CHAPTER 7

RICK LET SOME OF THE OTHER MEN PULL SPARKS'S BODY OFF THE helicopter. He turned to leave, but Sergeant Zeller took hold of his arm and walked him away from the team. Then Zeller stopped and looked him in the face. "Ward, you did all right until things got hot. It wasn't wrong for you to drop down when the fire started, but you have to know what's going on around you and respond. If we'd all hunkered down and stayed the way you did, the gooks would have overrun us. I know this is all new to you, and I was glad you got up and fired your weapon, but you gotta react faster next time."

"All right, Sergeant."

"Do you want to stay with us?"

Rick thought of saying no. But he didn't know what he really wanted right then, so instead he said, "Yes. I'll be fine."

"You were good at keeping sound discipline, better than most new guys, but I gotta tell you, I don't know if you can make it with us. I'll give you one more try."

"Okay. There for a minute, I reacted without thinking. Next time I'll keep my head." Rick was just talking. He had no idea what he would do "next time." The only thing he was sure of was that he'd rather not face another day in the jungle. And he still hadn't found out what the nights were like.

"Ward, you gotta know, Sparks is the first man I've lost. I've had two wounded, but this was my first KIA. You don't need to think this stuff happens all the time. We take pride in bringing our men back from these patrols."

Zeller had seemed cold, even hard until now, but Rick saw what was in his eyes. He looked older than he had an hour or two earlier. He'd looked at Sparks's torn-up body, the same as Rick had, and no doubt he felt responsible.

"All right. Get a shower. We got four days to rest now, and then we'll be back out there again."

Rick was numb. He thought he'd been well trained, but he hadn't known that death happened on a normal day like this—and then things went forward, same as always. He hadn't known about bodies, how easily they ripped and broke apart. Who was he kidding? He couldn't do this. He wanted to take off running, hide out somewhere, figure out some way to catch an airplane headed for the States.

But somehow he did manage to get cleaned up. The shower was actually a big canvas bag suspended in the open air, full of cold water. He felt a little better standing under the stream. When he got back to his tent, he lay on his cot. He wanted to sleep, but he was wide awake, and he was shaking. He found himself recalculating how many days he had left on his tour of duty. For the first time, he seriously doubted he'd ever get home.

He wondered what it was like to die. He didn't know what he believed about that, but he hated to think of the nothingness, of never doing the things he wanted to do, of never seeing his mother or sister again. It was all more than he knew how to deal with. He found himself fighting not to scream.

He'd heard stories about guys going crazy out there in the jungle—just losing it. He'd never thought himself capable of something like that, but now he wasn't sure. He'd known fear before, but nothing like he'd felt today. Lying in those ferns, his body had locked up and he'd had no control over himself. No one had known, because of all the sweat, but he had actually wet his pants.

Kent had come back from the shower. He sat down on his cot. "Are you okay?"

"Sure."

"It's the first time I've seen one of our men get killed. I'm not doing that well, if you want to know the truth. No one is. Sparks was a great guy. I know what this is going to do to his mother and his brothers."

Rick noticed that Kent hadn't mentioned a father. But he didn't ask about that. He didn't want to know any more about Sparks. He didn't want to talk to Kent, either.

"Rick, some new guys come over here all excited about war. You know what I mean? They've watched too many movies. That's all Whiley was trying to say to you in the slick. It's serious business. But he only did that because he was having a hard time himself. I don't know if you looked at him, but he was crying all the way back."

Rick thought he'd known that, but he'd never looked right at Whiley. What he'd heard was Whiley cursing over and over, calling the gooks all the names he could think of.

"I don't like Whiley," Kent said, "and J. D.'s just barely a human being, if you ask me. He's treated me like garbage from the day I got here. But both of them will look out for you in the woods. You don't ever have to worry about that."

"Yeah, I guess that's right." Rick hadn't opened his eyes. He wished that Kent would go away.

"Most of our missions aren't like that one, Rick. Lots of times we make no contact at all, and usually we're the ones who set up the ambush. It's just too bad it happened your first time out."

Rick didn't say anything. Kent waited for a time and then he lay back on his own cot. But he wasn't breathing steadily, not like a guy falling asleep. Rick had heard the nervousness in his voice and knew he was still tense. He might as well ask what he needed to know. "How are we supposed to go back out there in a few days?"

Kent let his breath blow out. "We just do. One thing you learn is not to think ahead. Sometimes I hate the time back here more than the time in the field. In the woods you feel connected to the other men, and you deal with what you have to do. Back here, you think how long a year is. Every day I pray for strength, and that's how I get through—one day at a time."

Rick hadn't prayed since he was a little boy, when his mother used to kneel by his bed with him and help him say, "Now I lay me down to sleep." But he thought he'd prayed out there in the jungle. At least some words of that kind had gone through his mind. "My mom used to tell me that people have a soul. But Sparks's body was just—I don't know—like a big lump of hamburger."

"That's all a body is when the spirit's gone. It's dust, and it goes back to the dust."

"So what do you believe? That there's a life after death?"

"Yes, I do."

Rick didn't know whether he believed that. "Do you think someone like Whiley is scared of dying?"

"Sure he is. All that toughness is an act. Right now, every guy on our team, including Whiley, is figuring out some way to pull himself together."

"What were you thinking today—you know, when the firefight broke out?"

"I don't know. I go on automatic. I do what I've been trained to do. After, I try not to think about it, but I can't help it."

None of that sounded right. Rick knew what he'd felt, and it wasn't what he'd expected. He knew too that Whiley was upset only because a friend was dead. None of the rest of it bothered him. The fact was, Whiley and J. D. *loved* to kill gooks. It was like hunting to them, like killing rats. They laughed about that kind of stuff all the time.

After a while Rick could hear that Kent was drifting off to sleep. But Rick couldn't relax. There was way too much stuff running around in his head, and there was no one he could talk to. So he dug out his notebook.

I feel like I know something now. Something I don't like. I got into my first firefight today and I was so scared I wanted to dig myself into the ground. It took everything I had to make myself stand up. But when I saw someone out there, I wanted to kill him—so he couldn't shoot me. Except it was more than that. I felt crazy for a few minutes. Someone was trying to kill me and I went wild to get him before he got me.

I didn't expect anything like that. I've wondered at times about aiming my rifle at a guy and pulling the trigger. But this wasn't like that. I didn't care anything about him. I wanted to destroy him. And I wanted to live.

I can't get Sparks out of my head. His face was torn apart and his jaw was hanging off so you could look into his throat, which was spilling out blood. All I could think was that some guy was happy when he did that. All our guys like to talk about wasting gooks, like it's a sport or something, and I hate that. But I was no better. I wanted to kill. Then it all got turned around when I had to look at Sparks. When you see a guy's guts coming out of his body, it's like the most real thing you've ever seen—it's the first time you find out a body is just a bunch of stuff, like anything else. But it's sort of not real either, because you tell yourself it just can't be like that. Everyone "discusses" the war back home, but to me, already that talk seems like a joke. No one out there in the jungle was thinking about fighting for freedom or any of those other things people talk about. You strip all the nice stuff off a guy, the act we all put on, and there's nothing much left—nothing to admire, anyway. Conrad had to go all the way up the Congo, and then he made it seem like the evil was sort of hidden and mysterious. But it's not like that. The dark is right there in front of you and you can get to it fast.

So is that what I came over here to learn? Is that my big insight that I can write about now—that a guy would rather kill than be killed? I could have figured that out at home. So how come I still can't breathe? I feel like I do know something new, and it's something I don't want to know. I don't want to tell anyone else, either. What good would it do?

Rick put the notebook away, and even though he didn't think he could, he finally slept—for twelve hours. But when he awoke in the morning, he didn't feel any better. He had dreamed and tossed all night. He had seen intestines in his dream, bouncing, vibrating, the way they had in the helicopter. And he had seen himself in the jungle, spinning around and around, trying to see who was behind him, the enemies spinning with him, out of sight.

Kent was up already. When he saw Rick sit up, he asked, "Do you want to go into town with me? We can look around for a while, maybe even take a swim in the ocean, and get a lobster dinner real cheap."

Rick wondered whether there wasn't someone else in the platoon he could make friends with. Back in California he never would have thought of hanging out with Kent. The guy was too old, for one thing. But Rick needed something to do. He didn't want to think about the stuff that had been in his head all night. "Okay," he said. "I want to take a shower first."

"Yeah, sure. We're in no hurry."

So Rick showered in cold water again and felt clean for a few minutes before the sweat came back. He ate breakfast in the mess tent, and then he and Kent walked out the camp gate together. The village was a little way off, but beat-up taxis and motorcycles with sidecars were waiting by the gate. The first taxi in line was a little black car of no make Rick had seen before. A man was standing by it—a very small guy, even by Vietnamese standards. "You want ride?" he asked, looking eager. "I give you cheap price."

"Sure," Kent said. Rick had wanted to walk, just to get moving, but he was still deadly tired. Maybe Kent was right to hire the taxi.

The driver had a stiff right leg, but he hurried back to his taxi and opened the door. "This good taxi. Very clean," he said. He sounded like some store clerk trying to impress a customer. Rick hated that kind of stuff.

As soon as the man got in the front and started his car, Kent said, "Driver, tell me your name."

Rick couldn't believe this guy. What did he care?

The driver looked over his shoulder. "*My* name?" he asked.

"Yes."

Rick thought the man said "chang-hwa," but Kent said, "Is it Trang? Trang Hoa?"

"Yes. You say good."

"I've been trying to learn some Vietnamese."

"What you can say? Bang, bang?"

Rick knew about that. In An Khe, he had heard the girls on the streets. "Hey, Joe, you want bang, bang? I love you long time. Two dollar."

"Oh, no," Kent was saying. "I just want to learn some of the language if I can." And then he said something in Vietnamese. Trang answered, and there was a short exchange before Kent said, "That's about all I can say."

Trang laughed. "So what you Joes want today? Good time? I get you good whiskey. Any kind of drink."

"We don't drink," Kent said.

"Speak for yourself, Kent."

Kent laughed.

"*You* want good fun?" Trang was saying, twisting to look at Rick, not Kent. "I know girls. Very clean. No VD."

104

"No," Rick said. He had heard the talk, knew how many of the men visited the brothels in town, but the idea bothered him.

Kent leaned forward. "Trang, what has the war done to you? How bad is it for your people?"

Trang turned to look back at them. "Not good for me. I fight in war. Vietcong soldier shoot me in knee. I come to city, drive taxi."

"What did you do before?"

"Grow rice. Cannot now."

"Your knee doesn't bend, does it?"

"No. No bend."

"So you can't work in the rice paddies?"

"Yes."

"Are you happy about American soldiers being here, or do you wish we would go home?"

"You good Joes."

Rick couldn't believe Kent. The locals couldn't be trusted; everyone said so. These people were hustlers, looking for a few bucks any way they could get them. A lot of them were Vietcong. The same guys who bowed and grinned and talked nice turned into sappers at night, crawling through the camp wires with explosives. Kent was like Rick's embarrassing uncle Frank back home, who always thought he had to talk to everyone. Kent probably wanted to create good relations on behalf of his country, or something like that, but that was stupid. Rick had seen how much these people hated Americans.

Trang asked again what Kent and Rick wanted. He said he could get black market weapons, ammo, gear. He could have suits made for them, very cheap. Kent just kept saying, "No, thanks," and laughing. "I'd like to get to know a few people in town," he said. "I want to get acquainted. It seems too bad to live here and never really understand the culture."

Trang didn't answer. Either he didn't understand or he thought Kent was as stupid as Rick did. He drove to the center of the town and parked at a little square. Phan Thiet was even more barren than most of the towns—all sand and tufts of grass and buildings that sagged from age. The only beauty came from the blue-green water in the bay. There was a horrible smell in the air—one Rick had noticed before in An Khe and sometimes at the camp, but it was more intense here.

"They make a fish sauce in Phan Thiet. It's called *nuoc mam*," Kent said. "That's what you're smelling." But he was now looking at Trang. He handed him a couple of army scrip dollars. "Is this enough?"

"Too much. You keep one. I give you ride every time. Take good care of you."

"No. You keep that. But please answer my question. Do you wish the war was over?"

"Yes. I wish."

"But what about Communism?" Rick asked. "You don't want the North to win, do you?"

Trang took a long look at Rick. "This was good country. I farm. I like."

Rick wasn't sure Trang had understood his question. "But if Ho Chi Minh wins the war, you'll have to be Communists. Wouldn't that be bad for you?"

"I don't know this. I drive taxi now. No farm."

"So you don't care if the Communists win?"

Trang looked away. "You want eat good food? I show you good place."

"You can answer," Kent said. "Would it be better if all us Americans left you alone?"

Trang's face changed as though he had dropped his mask. "Too many Joes. Not good here. Better if girls farm rice. Not bang bang for Joes."

"Your people have been fighting all your life, Trang," Kent said. "Are you tired of so much war?"

Why did Kent have to ask that? He was like some sort of social worker.

"Yes. Tired." His eyes deepened, an immense sadness behind them.

That surprised Rick. He hadn't expected an honest answer.

"I'm sorry," Kent told him. "I'm sorry the war ever started."

"Yes," Trang said. "Yes." Then he added, "You good Joe." But he was looking toward the street now. A little girl was crossing. He waved and spoke to her. The little girl was beautiful, with perfect skin and lovely black eyes. She was clean, in shorts and a little silk blouse, bright blue. She wasn't like the kids who filled the streets in the big cities and begged for cigarettes and candy or sold themselves to the soldiers.

Trang looked back at Kent and Rick. "This my— how you say?—do-tah."

"Daughter?"

"Yes. Daw-ter."

"She's beautiful."

Trang smiled. "Yes. She tell me, come home. Eat."

"All right," Kent said. "You go get something to eat. But thanks for talking to us. We'll watch for you—and always ride with you. We want to be your friend."

Trang nodded and made a little bow, but Rick thought he seemed skeptical. "Yes. Very good," he said. He walked to a little house on the opposite side of the square. The building was constructed of a crude brick that appeared stacked, not mortared, with a rough wood door and a roof of corrugated steel. Trang opened the door and he and his daughter went inside.

Kent shook his head. "I really need to get to know some of these people," he said. "We can't come over here and say that we're helping them if we don't even know what they want."

Rick was annoyed. How could Kent be so stupid? "What they want is to get their hands into our pockets."

"Sure they do. But is that so bad? They're trying to

survive. Back home, we'd give them credit for being 'enterprising.'"

Rick didn't know about that. Trang seemed all right, but maybe he was just like the ones out there in the woods—the ones firing those AK-47s. Maybe it was someone like Trang who had shot Sparks. Rick wasn't at all sure he could figure out which of the Vietnamese he should like and which ones he was better off killing. But all the questions made his head hurt. What he wanted was to eat now, then look around, go for a swim—do anything but think.

CHAPTER 8

DURING THE NEXT THREE DAYS RICK ASKED HIMSELF OVER AND OVER whether he could stand to go back to the jungle. At least a dozen times he decided he'd have to ask for a transfer out of Charlie Company, but the thing was, going back to the 173rd didn't sound any better, and he didn't have the option of asking for a desk job or a return to the States. It was easier to let inertia carry him into another patrol than to make a decision to leave. As it turned out, the next mission was frightening but uneventful, and he got through it all right. After that, it was easier to keep going than to leave these guys he was getting acquainted with. And even though he hated to admit it, he found himself depending on Kent.

Three months dragged by. Rick had arrived at the beginning of the hot, dry season, in February, when the heat had been terrible, but April and May were worse. It was close to the end of May now and Rick had 268 days to go, but the number could have been a thousand, the way it sounded in his brain. At least he could feel good about his developing skills as a "Lurp." The pattern had stayed pretty much the same. The men on his team would insert into the jungle, stay three or four days—unless they made contact—and then return to camp for about four days. Since the disastrous mission when Sparks had been killed, not all that much had happened. A couple of ambushes had produced a total body count of five NVA for the two-four team, but most of the insertions had led to nothing but exhausting hikes up and down mountains, with no success. Everyone was getting uptight about that. Prestige in the company came to those who got kills. Whiley and J. D. were itching for action, and Zeller seemed frustrated by the cold Areas of Operation the team had been pulling. Another man had been transferred to the two-four—an experienced guy named Roger Haws, better known as "Bulldog." He carried a collection of ears he had cut off NVA kills. The day he arrived, he'd shown them to Rick with an eerie delight in his pale eyes, and said, "I only got seven. I need a few more to make a good necklace." Rick had laughed and told Bulldog he was impressed, but he didn't touch the ears, and he didn't have much to do with the guy after that.

Rick hated humping the hills. Sometimes he

wanted to make contact or spring an ambush just to get extracted sooner. But when his team got its kills, he didn't like to look at the Vietnamese who lay dead in the kill zones. He'd tell himself he was only doing what he had to do; he wasn't the one who had thought up this war. But he didn't feel the way the other men did. When a team returned with a good body count, the men were excited, boisterous, almost crazy in the way they got high and celebrated. Some of them seemed addicted to combat. Haws wasn't the only one who collected ears. Rick had even seen souvenir fingers.

Each of the platoons in the company had death cards that the men carried and placed on enemy kills. The one for Rick's platoon said, "Satan's Playboys, From Hell We Rise, We Kill for Fun." He'd heard men say that they wished they could insert into college campuses back in the States and tear up a crowd of protesters with an M-60. Charlie Rangers mocked the idea of the peace sign, which a lot of the regular troops liked to flash. They'd hold up three fingers instead of two, to make a *W*, meaning "War."

But worst for Rick was hearing the men talk about the enemy soldiers they "wasted." What no one ever said was that this killing had some purpose—that Communism had been dealt a blow or that an evil had been corrected. Even worse, the men's hatred always came out in racist language. The gooks were "little rats" or "monkeys," and they slithered through the jungle like snakes. Rick hated that kind of talk. He'd gone to schools that had a fair number of minorities, and even though his close friends were almost all white, he believed in the civil rights movement. Here, though, even blacks and Hispanics slurred the Vietnamese. Rick thought it was probably true that you couldn't trust the Vietnamese, but that didn't mean they were animals.

What Rick longed for was a justification for what he was doing. His uncle Frank had been in World War II and he had known what he was fighting for, but Rick had merely come to have an experience, and he was gradually realizing how wrong that attitude was. He'd believed before he left home that the war made no sense, but he hadn't realized how evil it would feel. Still, Rick never expressed any of these feelings. He was learning to talk like a Charlie Ranger. If a guy wasn't "bad" and didn't show it, he was in for abuse, and new guys had to pick up the swagger fast or they were rejected. Kent was the exception. He took more abuse than anyone. He handled it silently when it didn't go too far, and then stood up and told a guy to shut his mouth when it did. He was big and muscular, and something in him seemed to say, "Don't try to find out how tough I can be." Early on, he'd saved a man's life by packing him through a hot landing zone with bullets flying past him. It was the story men in the company always told about Kent, and it was exactly the kind of thing soldiers respected.

Rick couldn't create that kind of image for himself, so he worked hard at being one of the guys. He used filthy language, worse than he'd ever used in his life. He laughed at their disgusting stories about killing and mutilating. He didn't drink much and didn't smoke weed, and the men badgered him about that, but he took his worst ribbing for hanging around Preacher. He knew very well that he'd be better off to take up with some of the younger guys, but Kent was the only man he could talk to honestly, so he clung to the guy— and then did everything he could to show the men that he wasn't like him.

"I can't figure you out," Rick told Kent one night when most of the guys were sitting around a bonfire outside, getting drunk. "How can a religious guy like you go out in the jungle and kill?"

They were both lying on their cots. There hardly seemed a breath of air in the tent with the heat lingering into the night. "I don't know. I tell myself that I have to honor my country and fight because our leaders feel the war is worthwhile, but it's hard to buy into that. There's really no such thing as South Vietnam. It's just something we invented. There were supposed to be free elections after the French got beaten, but we didn't let that happen because we knew the Communists would win. The government we set up is completely corrupt, and their army has no commitment to defend it. All we've done is force Ho Chi Minh to look for help from the Chinese, and that's linked him up with other Communist countries more than he ever would have. In a few years we'll be gone, and after all the killing and all the destruction, there'll be one Vietnam—and it'll be Communist."

It was what Judy had always said. "A lot of the guys say we're not fighting the war right. We need to go bomb Hanoi the way we bombed Berlin in World War II. My recruiter back home told me that before I ever came over here."

"And if we did that, who would we do it for?"

"To win the war and keep the North from taking over the South."

"Rick, we've dropped as many bombs on Vietnam as we dropped in all of World War II, and it hasn't ended the war. Hitler was trying to take over Europe and we drove him back. But this is a civil war. In fact, it's not even that. We're the ones who came in and decided what was best for this country—and not enough of the Vietnamese people are with us. You can't win a war that way."

Rick looked up into the darkness. The firelight from outside was casting moving shadows on the canvas tent top, like trees in a wind. "So if you think the war is wrong, why do you keep fighting?" This was the real question he'd wanted to ask.

"I don't think a guy has the right to choose when he'll honor his government and when he won't. I got called up to do this and I hate it, but I'm going to do the best I can. What I don't want to do is get blood-thirsty. In the Scriptures, that's the evil of war: when men start to like what they're doing."

"The guys in our platoon like it."

"I'm not so sure about that. They like the adrena-line rush. But they pretend the enemy isn't human, and I don't think they'll be able to tell themselves that forever."

Rick wasn't sure. He didn't think Whiley, or J. D., or especially Bulldog would ever have second thoughts about what they were doing.

"I wish I hadn't had to come here," Kent said softly. "I've seen things I'll never be able to get out of my head. I feel a sadness inside me sometimes that's like a sick-ness. I'm not sure I'll ever get rid of it. I spent two years trying to bring happiness to people, and now I feel like I've canceled out any good I've done in this world."

Rick understood that. But he knew he couldn't let that much darkness inside himself. He had nine months to survive, and he could do it only on the army's terms. He decided never to talk to Kent about this kind of stuff again. He'd hoped that Kent might have found some justification that Rick could grab on to. But this kind of talk didn't help at all. Whether Rick felt good about it or not, he was better off taking on the attitude of the other men. If he didn't want to get killed, he needed to be the one to do the killing.

Two days later Rick was up again, packing his ruck-sack, testing it so it would ride high on his shoulders and not rub into his back. He used a camo stick to paint his face, picked up his weapon from the Connex lockers, and then caught a truck with the other men to the helipad. Every nerve was awake and active when he headed into the woods. All concentration was on the task at hand, and in some ways that was good. It was always when he was lying around thinking that he got himself into trouble. But in the jungle he watched and waited, concentrated on every step he took, and he felt good about the guys on his team. They did their jobs and watched out not just for them-selves but for everyone. He felt tied to them then, felt a sort of love for men he didn't even like.

For two days the team hiked the jungle, made no contact, and saw no sign of enemy presence. Bulldog Haws was walking point on the third morning, heading up a hill through a clearing in the brush. For the first time Rick was pulling slack, behind Haws. He felt good about that, since it showed that Sergeant Zeller now had some confidence in him. Haws was doing everything right, moving slowly, watching the tree line, checking the ground for booby traps.

Rick was glancing to his right, scanning the tree

line, when he heard a *pop*. He looked ahead to see Haws on the ground.

"Get down, Ward," Zeller whispered. Rick hit the ground. "Haws, are you hit?" Zeller called.

"No. He missed me."

"We've got a sniper," Zeller said. "We've got to get out of this clearing. Let's go."

The men jumped up and charged forward, still in a line. Just as Haws was reaching the tree line, Rick heard another little ping, and Haws dropped again. Rick knew that Bulldog was hit this time. He ran past and took the point as he was trained to do, and then he saw the sniper. The man had dropped from a tree in his tan uniform, and he was turning, bringing his rifle around. The muzzle flashed as Rick dropped to the ground and released a burst of fire from his M-16 at the same moment. The man's chest exploded and he fell backward against the tree, then slumped to the ground.

Nothing moved after that. Rick was watching frantically, scanning the trees, but there was not a sound out there except for Bulldog, rasping and moaning. Someone was moving, and Rick figured it was Sergeant Zeller, but he didn't look back. Snipers usually worked alone, but he wasn't going to assume anything right now.

Rick heard Zeller working on Bulldog, ripping his shirt open. After a few seconds Zeller said, "Haws is hit bad. J. D., call in a sitrep. Get gunships and a dustoff in here, and an extraction slick for the rest of us. We'll drop back to the LZ we set up for E and E. Whiley, check out that gook. Richards, help me get Haws out of here."

All this language was second nature to Rick now. A "sitrep" was a situation report. "E and E" was escape and evasion, and before every patrol, during visual reconnaissance from the air, the CO and the team leader picked out an escape landing zone so that a helicopter could land and extract the team. But now the site would also serve as a landing zone for a dustoff—a medevac helicopter to get help to Bulldog as quickly as possible.

Whiley ran ahead and searched the sniper for papers or maps, but he took longer than Rick thought he needed to. Finally Whiley grabbed the soldier's automatic rifle and ran back toward the team. By then Kent and Zeller were walking fast, carrying Haws. Now, with the team moving back, Rick became rear security, walking backward and watching for an enemy response. A sniper was not likely to be too far from his unit, so the fire could attract enemy troops.

The team moved quickly, abandoning sound discipline and working their way to a trail in the bottom of the valley. Once they hit the trail, they ran hard and steady, but the LZ wasn't far off. It was a bomb crater that had opened up a clearing in the woods. The men reached the tree line and then spread out and waited.

J. D. called in another situation report and got the word that a medevac was two mikes out and was coming in with two gunships. A slick would follow. That sounded good to Rick. His eyes were still on the trail.

Rick soon heard the whomping sound of the helicopter rotors. Zeller threw out a smoke grenade and red smoke began to rise. "Have them confirm the color," Zeller whispered. J. D. got back on the handset for the confirmation.

The two Cobras came in low, right over the top of the team. They tore up the jungle with their miniguns, but Rick couldn't hear or see any return fire from the ground. The dustoff came over the trees and descended into the narrow LZ. Before it was down, Zeller and Kent were running Haws to the door, where the medics on board pulled him in. The dustoff lifted and not a minute later, the slick descended. The Cobras were still shooting up the trail and the jungle around it.

Rick ran with the others. They boarded from both sides, and suddenly they were in the air sliding over the top of the trees, then lifting fast. Rick felt as though he could finally breathe. All the men were drawing in air, the same as he was. Zeller yelled above the whine of the turbine, "Haws should make it. He got hit high in the chest, but we got the bleeding stopped."

Rick breathed even better. He was sitting close to the door. He wanted the air from outside to fill him up, cool him off.

Whiley leaned over and shouted in Rick's ear, "You got some payback on that gook. Nice shooting."

For the first time, Rick let himself remember—the little man's chest bursting, blood spattering. Rick had fired his weapon during ambushes, but he'd never actually known for sure that he had killed a man.

"You're blooded now, Ward. You're a man. I got something off that gook. It's yours, if you want it."

Rick knew what was coming. He tried to turn away. But there was Whiley's hand in front of him, holding a wrinkled and red little piece of flesh. "No. No. I don't want that!" Rick shouted. He hit Whiley's hand and the ear dropped onto the steel floor and slid in its blood.

J. D. grabbed it and held it up, laughing. Kent grabbed J. D.'s arm, but J. D. tossed the ear back at Rick before Kent could stop him. Rick's hand jerked up. The ear glanced off his hand and hit his face, then dropped into his lap. Frantic, Rick grabbed it and tossed it out the door.

Whiley was roaring with laughter. "That's all right. You don't have to keep it. But you got some blood on you. That's what you needed. You'll be all right now."

Rick looked down at his hand, bloody from the ear

of the man he'd killed. He swallowed hard. He wiped his face with his sleeve, and then he slid closer to the door, into the blast of air, but he glanced to see that Kent was screaming into J. D.'s face.

Rick looked away. He concentrated on the horizon, the distant blue of the sea. But the thought had already come to him: Who was that man he'd killed? He hadn't looked very old, but it was hard to tell with the Vietnamese. Did he have a family? A mother? A little sister?

But it was stupid to ask questions like that. "Don't think about that," he said to himself out loud, into the wind. "Don't think. Just don't think."

CHAPTER 9

WHEN THE HELICOPTER LANDED BACK AT THE CAMP, RICK JUMPED off and started to walk to his tent. But Sergeant Zeller called, "Ward, wait a minute."

Zeller summoned the other men, and then he stood in front of Rick. Zeller was much shorter and had to look up at Rick, but at that moment he seemed huge. The rest of the team gathered around them.

"What you guys did up there in the slick was wrong. I don't want to see anything like that again," Zeller said. "Whiley, as far as I'm concerned, there's no place on this team for that kind of behavior. We don't like it when the dinks do that kind of stuff to our men, and I've told you before, I don't tolerate it on this team."

Whiley didn't say anything.

"But I'll tell you what's worse," Zeller said. "We had a man go down out there today. If you men can see that happen and then fool around like that, it makes me wonder what's wrong with you."

"Come on, Sarge," J. D. said. "I don't know what Preacher was so mad about. We were just—"

"Shut your mouth, Duffy." Zeller stopped and cursed. "Ward did his job today, and he did it well. He's turned into a first-rate soldier. There was not one reason to belittle him. You don't want to find out what I'll do if this doesn't stop."

"It wasn't meant to make fun of him, Sarge," Whiley said. He reached his hand out to Rick. "Ward, I didn't mean nothing like that. That ear was a badge of honor. You stepped up front and took that little gook out. I'm proud of you."

Rick shook Whiley's hand, and then J. D.'s. When Kent patted him on the back, though, it seemed just a little too fatherly. It would only make things worse with the others. So Rick stepped away from Kent, and then he walked back to the tent with the team, not saying much. He felt numb. What he wanted more than anything was a shower. He stood in the water for as long as possible, but he tried not to think about what had happened. He tried not to think at all.

When Rick got back to his tent, Whiley and J. D. had pulled off their boots and wiped the camouflage from their faces. They were talking to some men from another team. Rick stayed out of the conversation and busied himself with getting dressed.

A new guy named Bernie stepped toward Rick. "Hey, nice going," he said. "Whiley was just tellin' us what you did today."

Rick shook Bernie's hand. A corporal named Blodgett joined them. "It's good you took care of that gook," Blodgett said. "Haws is a good man."

Rick shook Blodgett's hand and tried to sound strong. "We gotta kill a lot more. One gook's not enough payback for a downed Ranger."

"That's exactly right," Blodgett said. Rick saw Whiley nodding approval. But Rick felt his hands shaking and he knew he had to get away from these guys. He went back to his cot and pulled on his boots. Kent had returned from the shower and was getting dressed. Rick didn't want to talk to him, either.

"Hey, Ward!" Whiley yelled at Rick. "We finally got a name for you. You're 'Killer' from now on. I want to buy you a beer—show there's no hard feelings. Me and J. D., we gotta get cleaned up. Then let's go down to the Enlisted Men's Club and tip a few."

Rick couldn't think what to say. He mumbled, "Okay. I'll catch you a little later," and then he got up and left. He wasn't walking fast; he didn't want to bring any attention to himself, but he was looking for a place where no one could find him.

"Rick, wait up."

It was Kent, the last person he wanted to see right now. "I'm just gonna . . . I don't know . . . walk or something," Rick said.

"Do you mind if I go with you?"

"Actually, yeah. I just want to clear my head a little." He swallowed. He had to get away. Any minute he was going to lose it.

But Kent put his hand on Rick's shoulder. "I know what you're going through."

Rick didn't want to be seen like this. He didn't need to be consoled like he was a little kid. He shook Kent off and kept walking, but now he could feel his chest shaking. He breathed hard, willed himself not to cry. He didn't know why Kent wasn't listening to him. The guy was still keeping up alongside him.

"The first time I killed a man," Kent said, "I had to search him. I thought I was all right, but when I got about two steps away from him I started vomiting."

Rick didn't answer. He kept walking. The road was lined with ugly green tents, all of them covered with red dust.

"The thing is, Rick, it's good that it wasn't easy for you. It shouldn't be. You need to hope that you never do get used to it. Some guys—"

"Kent, this isn't what I need right now." He stopped and turned toward Kent. "I know you want to help, but I just want to get away for a while." Suddenly all the emotion was thumping in his body again, pounding with the beat of his heart, and he couldn't stand it. He strode away hard this time. What he really wanted was to run—run so hard he filled up his head and chest with pain and left no room for anything else. He wanted to run from this camp, wanted to run all the way home, wanted to leave this whole mess behind him. He wanted to play volleyball on the beach and hang out with his friends. He wanted to see Judy, hold her—go back to that time when things had been good between them.

He passed some men who watched him go by, curious, maybe because they could see the tears that were filling his eyes. He kept going until he reached the wire at the end of the camp, and then he stood there looking across the sand, the elephant grass beyond that, and the deep green of the distant jungle.

He was breathing hard and sweat was running from his hair, down his face. He told himself to take deep breaths. He wasn't crazy. He wasn't going to crack up. He wasn't that kind of guy. He needed to clear his head a little, that was all, and then he would go drink a beer with Whiley and J. D. But his next thought was that he'd have to go back after that—to the tent, and then to the jungle. Suddenly he couldn't stop himself. The tears came, and then the sobs.

He fought for control. He didn't cry very long. But he continued to stare off at the jungle. He wished he could have one night away from the tent and the men and all the talk—one night in his room at home with his music and his notebook. But he had to be a man. Soldiers killed. He'd always known that. There was something wrong with him if he couldn't deal with that.

He heard someone come up behind him, and he knew it had to be Kent again.

"If you want me to get lost, I will," Kent said.

Rick turned, thinking that he'd tell the guy to do just that. Instead he ducked his head and said, "No. That's okay." He looked past Kent, down the dirt road. No one was looking their way.

"You're wondering who that man was, aren't you? The one you shot."

"No, I'm not. I'm not going to do that. We're soldiers. We do what we have to do."

Kent shook his head. "One time after a firefight, I saw one of our men roll up in a ball on the ground. He'd been one of the real tough guys in our platoon, always talking about getting his kills, and then one day he'd had enough. They put him on a medevac and shipped him out. We never saw him again."

"That's him, not me."

"I know. But I've seen that a lot. This hunt-and-kill stuff is hard on all of us."

"You keep saying that, Kent, but I don't buy it. Most of these guys have never had so much fun in their lives. They'll go home and talk about what big-shot killers they were."

"Some of them will. But vet hospitals back home are filling up with guys who can't live with themselves now. Everyone has something inside himself that says that wrong is wrong. We know that killing another human being is disgusting, no matter what the reason."

"No way. I'm not going to think that way, Kent. I didn't do anything wrong. And I don't want to talk about it. All that does is mess me up."

"That's fine—if you can handle it that way."

Rick stared at Kent. He couldn't figure the guy out. He started to walk back to the tent. He was going to drink some beer—no matter how much he hated the stuff. A lot of beer.

"What are you going to do with your life, Rick?" Kent asked.

Rick didn't want to talk about that, either. "I don't know." He walked for a time, and then, just to avoid another question, he asked, "What about you?"

"My dad wants me and my brother to take over our farm. But I'm not sure I want to do that."

"You don't seem like a farmer."

"What do I seem like?"

"A college professor or something like that."

Kent laughed. "Well, we'll see. I've got a degree in psychology, and I might want to do graduate work. I've thought about teaching. First, though, I've got to get home in one piece. What about you? You're planning to go to college, aren't you?"

"I don't know." He walked again, vowing to say nothing more, but then admitted, "I've always wanted to be a writer. That's part of why I joined the army— to have some experiences." Kent smiled at that. Suddenly Rick felt like a little kid. An idiot. "I was also having trouble with my dad," he added quickly. "I wanted to get away from him as much as anything."

"What do you mean, trouble?"

"I don't know. He likes to run people's lives. He treats my mom like she's nothing. He tells me how worthless I am. I guess you don't know anything about stuff like that."

"Not really. Dad expected us to work hard—you know, get up early to do our chores—but he was the kind of guy who would give me a big hug and a kiss, no matter how old I got."

Tears filled Rick's eyes again; he hardly knew why, but it occurred to him that his sadness hadn't really started in Vietnam. He blinked, took a breath, and said, "I guess you're pretty close to your mom, too? And your brother and little sisters?"

"Yeah. Brent and I, we used to get into it once in a while. We'd argue about who was supposed to milk that morning and all that kind of stuff. But we'd get into trouble together, and that made us feel like partners."

"Trouble? What kind?"

"We weren't supposed to smoke, but we tried it a few times. One time Dad caught us rolling our own cigarettes down behind our old tool shed." Kent laughed. "And we used to drive down to Smithfield and get into fights. That's how farm boys prove they're tough. Dad didn't think much of that—especially when we came back with a black eye or something like that. We got chased out of town by a sheriff one time, and the sheriff knew Dad's car. He called Dad, and boy, we heard about that."

"I didn't think you ever did things like that."

"Well . . . you know . . . I was young. Before my mission, I didn't think much about what I believed. I just tried to get away with a few things."

"Were your sisters like that too?"

"No. Not so much. Ginny used to sneak out to go with a boy Mom and Dad didn't like, but she finally figured out they were right about him. She would always come to me to talk about those things. Both my sisters did that. Mom, too. I think Mom's the smartest person I know. She's a history teacher at our high school. The two of us used to talk about *every-thing.*"

"My mom and I are pretty close too, but my dad is stealing the life out of her. She tries to be happy—for us kids—but she really isn't."

Kent nodded. He hesitated and then he said what Rick had been thinking. "We're supposed to be men, but we're all just boys over here. We bring all that stuff from home with us."

"Yeah." Rick looked down at his feet. His boots were worn. So were his fatigues. He wasn't a new guy anymore, but he was still Rick Ward, from Long Beach. It was hard to believe that he could go out on enough patrols to get a whole year behind him, hard to believe he would ever go home, hard to imagine who he would be by then. "I came over here wanting to prove to myself that I'm a man, but I think maybe I'm proving just the opposite."

"If cutting off a dead man's ear proves you're a man, I don't want to be one."

"I guess that's right. But let's not talk about any of that stuff. I need to get it out of my head."

"Sure."

Rick decided not to go to the EM Club, even though that would have made a good impression with some of the men in the platoon. Instead he wrote a letter to Roxie, and then one to his mother. He told them both that things were fine. He'd written before about the heat and the stench, and living in a tent, so he didn't have much more to add. He told Roxie to help their mother, to talk to her and keep her cheered up. He told his mother about Kent, who was being sort of a big brother to him, so she shouldn't worry about him. He thought of writing to Judy, but he'd written twice before and she hadn't answered. So he got out his notebook. He'd been avoiding it for a while, but he had to admit the truth somewhere.

When I came over here, I knew I didn't want to kill anyone, but I figured I could do it if I had to. Today I did kill a man. It happened in a second, and I didn't have time to think, so it wasn't hard. All my training kicked in, and he was dead and I was alive. The guy was a sniper, and he got one of our guys, so he had to know we'd shoot back at him. That's how it is. That's what I have to remember. I don't know if he was some gung-ho Communist and happy to die for his country or if he just did what someone told him to do. In a way, it doesn't matter—he's dead either way. I didn't kill him because I loved my country. It was just what we do.

The first time I fired my weapon over here, I was all crazy to stay alive. I thought I knew some things about myself after that. But this time, after it was over, I started to think about who the guy was. So it all seems different. And maybe what I thought I knew wasn't the whole story. But I can't say for sure what I know. What surprised me was that it would all be so cold—at least when it happened. It was only after, on the helicopter, when I started to think about it. One of our guys cut the sniper's ear off and wanted to give it to me. That bothered me at first just because it was so bloody, but later I kept remembering it, and that's when I started to feel sick.

*What I remembered was that it dropped down
onto my lap, and it looked human. It was him.
The guy wasn't just some sniper. He was a man.
He had a mom back home, probably brothers
and sisters, and maybe even a wife and kids. I
thought about that on the slick and for a little
while after, but I'm not going to anymore. Maybe
it was wrong to come over here to see some
things I could write about, but I was a dumb kid
when I made that decision, and it's too late to do
anything about it. I just have to remind myself,
the guy could have killed me just as easy as I
killed him. He was the one who died, but that's
just how things happened to work out. It's not
my fault. I'm not going to let it bother me all my
life. I just refuse to let that happen. That's what
makes guys crazy, I'm sure, going home and
thinking about everything.*

Rick put the notebook away and lay back on his
cot. Kent was sitting up writing some letters of his
own. Rick was dead tired and he wanted to sleep. He
closed his eyes, but when he did he saw the blood fly
like a halo around the man's body. He saw the chunks
of flesh hit the tree. He rolled over and pushed his face
against his arm, pressed it as hard as he could. He shut
his eyes tight, trying to see only black, but everything
was still red.

CHAPTER 10

RICK HAD A FITFUL, NERVOUS NIGHT, AND HE AWOKE EARLY. SOMETHING had changed inside him, and he didn't know what it was going to mean. He hated lying on his cot, fighting off his thoughts; he wanted to get up and do something. But he waited out the early hours until a few men started to stir, and then he got up and took a shower. When he got back, Kent was dressed.

"I'm thinking I'll go into town," Kent said. "Do you want to go?"

Rick didn't, really, but he'd been trying to think what he could do. He needed to clean his weapon and square away some of his gear, but that wouldn't take all day, and the four days ahead were terrifying to him. The men would be talking about the patrol, about Haws, about everything. It was a long time to keep from thinking.

"Yeah. I guess I'll go."

"I want to talk to Trang, if I can. I'd like to meet his wife."

"I don't see the point of that, Kent."

"I don't want to spend a year over here and never get to know these people."

"Well, I don't want to get to know them—not if we have to go back to the jungle."

Kent nodded. "I know what you mean," he said. He was bent over, lacing his boot. He was whispering because most of the men were still asleep. He tied the lace, and then he sat up straight and looked at Rick. "It feels like we have to hate them all, doesn't it? After a while, they all seem like the enemy, no matter what the politicians tell us. But we just can't think that way."

Rick stared at Kent. Who was the guy kidding?

"Okay. I know what you're thinking," Kent finally said. "But that's what I want to feel. I don't want to hate anyone—the ones in town *or* the ones in the woods."

It was too much. Rick had heard enough. He didn't say anything, but he shook his head in disbelief.

"Go to hell, all right?" Kent said.

"What?"

Someone at the opposite end of the tent mumbled, "Shut up, will you?" and Kent waited for a time. Finally he whispered, "Uncle Sam told me to kill my enemy, but Jesus Christ told me to love him. So what am I supposed to do? I want to follow Christ if I can. You know what I believe."

"No, I don't know. All you do is give me Sunday school lessons. I don't trust half the stuff you say."

Kent nodded. He looked away and worked on the other boot, taking his time. When he looked up, he seemed to know that Rick would still be watching him. "I know what's right," he said. "But I don't know how to do it. It just seems like there's more expected of me than I know how to give. I want to do what my country asks of me, but I don't want to kill, and I don't want to hate."

"I don't think about stuff like that."

"Yeah, you do."

It was Rick who was caught off guard this time. But of course, Kent was right. After a few seconds, Rick nodded. "So what do we do?"

"They're all the same people, Rick—even if we draw a line through their country and only kill the ones from the north side. I pray about this all the time, and the one thing I've got figured out is that I need to know them if I'm going to love them."

"Then what about killing them?"

"It doesn't change that."

Kent looked directly into his eyes, and Rick felt lost. He didn't want more on his shoulders. He wished he had made friends with Whiley and J. D., right from the beginning.

"So do you want to see if we can find Trang?" Kent asked.

Rick didn't. But he didn't say that. "All right."

When Rick and Kent walked through the camp gate, they looked for Trang's taxi, but it wasn't there, so they hired another driver. In town they looked for Trang again but didn't see him, so they walked across the square to his home. Chances were he was working, but Kent figured they could meet his wife and ask where he might be.

They knocked on the door and even called out, but it was a long time before someone answered. A pretty woman—Trang's wife, maybe—stood in the doorway. She seemed wary.

"Where is Trang?" Kent asked, speaking slowly.

But Rick could see that the woman didn't speak English. She said something back in Vietnamese. "I think she said he's asleep," Kent said. He tried his Vietnamese, but her look didn't change.

"What are you telling her?" Rick asked.

"I said 'friend,' I think. And then I said 'beautiful little girl,' so she would know we met her daughter. That's the only kind of stuff I can say, but I don't think she knows what I'm trying to get at."

The woman began to close the door, but Kent spoke quickly, again in Vietnamese.

She stopped, took a long look at Kent, and then motioned for them to come inside. They ducked to step under the door frame and into a little room. She gestured for them to stop, and then she walked through another door.

"What did you say?"

"I said, 'I love Trang.' It was all I could think of."

Rick shook his head in disbelief. Kent was strange.

But the woman had come back to the little room. She motioned for Kent and Rick to follow her into the next room. Trang was lying on the floor on a mat. He looked terrible. His arm was bound with strips of cloth holding a wooden splint. He was wearing pajamas made from a silky white cloth, but the fabric had been cut up the side on one leg—the one with the stiff knee. Rick could see that the leg was bandaged.

Trang's eyes were closed. Rick didn't want to wake him, but Trang slowly rolled his head toward Kent and Rick, and his eyes came open—or at least one of them did. The other was red and swollen shut.

Kent knelt down by him. "What happened, Trang? Were you in a wreck?"

Trang stared at Kent with his good eye, but it didn't seem to focus.

"What happened to you?" Kent asked again.

"Man beat me. He drunk. He say I cheat."

"Who was it?"

"Bad Joe."

Rick felt sick. "Your eye looks infected," he said.

Trang didn't seem to know the word. "Leg bad again," he said. "Very bad. Arm break."

"What about your eye?" Kent asked. "It looks sick."

"Yes. Eye bad."

Rick looked up at Trang's wife, then back at Trang. It was disgraceful to think that some American had beaten up on Trang. "Do you have medicine?" he asked.

"No medicine."

"What can we do?" Rick asked Kent.

Kent stood. He looked at the woman and asked her something in Vietnamese.

"Vo Thi," she said.

Kent was pulling his wallet from his pocket. He took out some of the Army scrip the men received as pay. It was valuable on the black market. "Vo Thi, take this. You can buy food." He made a motion with his hand toward his mouth. Then he looked down at Trang. "We'll get you medicine, Trang. We'll go back to the base and we'll come back with it today. I promise."

By then Rick had his own wallet out. He gave Vo Thi a ten-dollar bill.

Trang stared at Kent as though he had a hard time believing what was happening, but he said, "Thank you. Thank you."

Kent and Rick left and took a taxi back to the camp. Then they walked to the camp infirmary, another tent. The young medic, a corporal, sat at the desk just inside the entrance. He wanted to know what they needed. "We want to talk to a doctor," Kent said.

"Both of you, or—"

"It doesn't matter. We're not sick. We just need him to help us with something."

"The doctors are busy. If you don't have a medical problem, I can't go in there and—"

"Okay. I think I have a venereal disease," Kent said.

The corporal smiled. "That's what I thought. Why didn't you just say so? Do you both have a dose, or just—"

"Yeah. Me too," Rick said. "I need some antibiotics."

"Okay. Sit down. I'll get you in when I can."

It was more than half an hour before the medic asked Kent to step into the clinic. When Rick asked to go in at the same time, the corporal seemed to find that strange, but he let them go in together.

They passed another desk. Beyond it, in a long room, were several cots. Soldiers were lying on some of them. Men came back from the jungle with all kinds of skin diseases and fevers, and the infirmary was where they came to be treated. A doctor finally approached. He was a big man, but soft, his flesh seeming loose under the scrubs he was wearing. He was wearing a bulky pair of horn-rimmed glasses that had slipped down on his nose. His face was running with sweat. "What do you men need?" he asked.

Rick wondered what Kent would say to the guy. Men

usually talked about getting shots for their venereal diseases. But they needed pills they could take back to Trang.

But Kent didn't say a thing about VD now that they were inside. "We know a man in town who was beaten up by one of our soldiers. He's in bad shape; he's got an infection in his eye. He needs antibiotics or I hate to think what's going to happen to him."

"What are we talking about here?" the doctor asked. He used his index finger to push up his glasses. "Is this man Vietnamese?"

"Yes."

"Then we don't get involved. If someone gets hit by friendly fire, or if he steps on a land mine, we can treat that. But when a guy gets in a fight, that's not our problem."

"A drunk American beat him up," Kent persisted. "This man is a taxi driver, dirt poor. He's an ARVN vet who took a bad leg wound that keeps him from farming."

"Yes, well, that's his version of the story. If we started treating all the locals, we'd never be able to take care of our own men."

Rick was suddenly furious. "I don't get this," he said. "We complain about these people hating us, but the way we treat them, who can blame them? We're turning them all into Vietcong."

"I'm sorry, but I have my orders. I can't help you."

"Wait a minute," Kent said. "What if I have VD? And what if I don't like shots? Could you give me some pills for that?"

"We give shots."

"But you could put that in your report—that you gave me some pills. Or let's see, instead of VD, you can say it's for an infection I got in the jungle. I got a cut, and it got infected. That happens."

"I can't do that for every guy who comes in here with a story. We're not supposed to treat indigenous personnel." He removed his glasses, pulled a handkerchief from his pocket, and wiped the sweat from his forehead and nose.

"How many stories do you get? Have you *ever* been asked for something like this?"

The doctor didn't answer.

"Just prescribe something for me. How can that hurt?"

Rick expected the doctor to turn them away, but he cursed and then left the room for a moment. When he came back, he had an envelope with him. "Look, I put some pills in here. Stick them in your pocket and don't say anything to anyone about it."

"Thanks."

"Tell your friend to take three a day, with meals. Does he speak enough English so you can explain that to him?"

"Yeah, he does." Kent stuck out his hand. "Thanks a lot."

The doctor pushed up his glasses again and looked disgusted, but he shook Kent's hand before he walked away.

After that, Rick thought they'd be heading back to town immediately, but Kent said he wanted to talk to the guys in the platoon first. When they got to the tent, quite a few of the men were there. One group was playing cards and some others were sleeping, but Kent didn't hold his voice down.

"Hey, I need to talk to you men about something," he said. "We were in Phan Thiet and we found out about a really sad situation. One of the Vietnamese taxi drivers who waits outside the base got beat up by an American soldier. Rick and I know this guy, and he's a good man. He got shot in the knee fighting with ARVN, and he can't walk very well. Some drunk soldier busted him up and he's got a bad infection in his eye. We got him some medicine, but he has nothing to live on. Do some of you want to chip in with us to help him? He's a vet, and it was an American who messed him up. It seems like we ought to help him."

A staff sergeant named Pugmire—one of the team leaders—cursed without looking away from his cards. "Preacher, you're a bleeding heart. There are poor people and busted-up people all over this country. There's no way GIs can take care of all of 'em."

"I think this case is a little different."

"Yeah, well, let the guy complain to the army. The

government is shoveling money into this country all the time. No reason your buddy can't pick up a little of that."

"There's no program for anything like this. We talked to one of the docs at the infirmary and he's been told not to do anything for someone like that."

"Pugmire," one of the young privates said, "you just took my whole paycheck. Hand over a little of that to Preacher and let him save the world."

"Not a chance. I earned that money fair and square—drawing that big deuce for three of a kind." All the men laughed.

"Look, you guys," Kent said. "I'm not asking for a lot. If everyone would chip in a dollar or two, that would go a long way for this man and his family."

Rick had thought that Whiley was sleeping, but now he sat up. "Preacher, I don't mind you being stupid, if that's what you want, but don't you *ever* break into my sack time. We're here to *kill* gooks, not to feed them. The guy's probably VC, and you don't have the brains to know it."

"That's right," a couple of the men said.

Pugmire added, "If you ask me, we oughta just nuke this whole country and then go home. That would stop any worries about starvation." The men laughed again.

Rick wasn't surprised by their reaction. What had Kent expected? But he could see that Kent was getting angry. Kent waited for a time, and then he said in a low, clear voice, "I've heard enough from the *scum* in this tent. I'm talking now to any *human beings* who can hear what I'm saying. Who's going to offer this man some help?"

Everyone looked up at Kent at the same moment. Nobody made a sound.

"Preacher, you watch your mouth," Whiley said, and he stood up.

Kent stepped in close and stared Whiley in the face. "If you don't want to be called scum, then don't act like it."

But now Zeller was up, moving between the two of them. "Hey, that's enough," he said. "We aren't going to have any of this."

Whiley stepped back, and to Rick's surprise, didn't try to push past Zeller. He was still staring at Kent, but he didn't look as angry as Rick had expected. By then most of the men were looking away. Pugmire mumbled, "Preacher, you're just lucky Whiley didn't rip your liver out and eat it," but there was more humor than anger in his voice.

A corporal named Williams, one of the few black guys in the platoon, had also gotten up from his cot. "I've got a few bucks you can have," he said. "And Gunner does, too." Gunderson—known as Gunner—protested, but Williams said, "Shake loose with a couple of bucks. You never spend a dime."

146

Gunderson got out his wallet and gave Williams some bills, and then Williams handed his and Gunderson's money to Kent. Three more men got out their wallets and handed bills over, but Whiley didn't say a word. When Rick and Kent left the tent, Rick looked back to see him lie down again. Rick could hardly believe what had just happened.

They took a taxi back to town. They gave the money to Trang with the antibiotics, and they made sure he understood how often to take the pills. Vo Thi cried and embraced them, and Rick felt better than he had at any time since he'd arrived in country.

They had to walk back to camp, since they'd both used nearly all their cash, but they didn't talk much.

They were almost back when Kent said, "I've got to talk to Whiley. I had no right to call him scum."

"Are you kidding me?"

"I'm supposed to be better than that, Rick. I talk about loving my enemy and I can't even love a guy who fights alongside me."

"I wouldn't apologize to him. He had it coming."

"Maybe. But I could have found a better way of saying it."

Rick laughed. "That was the best I ever liked you—when you stepped up nose to nose with him like that."

Kent smiled just a little, as though he liked the memory more than he wanted to. But after another few seconds, he said, "But I can't call the men names and then wonder why they think I'm self-righteous. I've got a long way to go if I'm ever going to be the man I want to be."

"I don't know about that, Kent. I think you're the best man I've ever met."

Kent stopped. He looked shocked. "Me?"

"Yes, you."

"Oh, Rick, you gotta get out more. You haven't met enough people."

But Rick thought he had.

CHAPTER 11

RICK AND KENT HAD BREAKFAST IN THE MESS TENT THE NEXT morning, and then they decided they would spend some time writing letters. Rick had never written to his dad, but he now felt he ought to make a little more effort to connect with him. He was sitting on his cot writing when Sergeant Woodward, one of the team leaders, stepped into the tent. Most of the men were still sleeping, a lot of them having gotten drunk the night before.

"Ward, Richards, Williams," Woodward said, "I need you to come with me. A sapper was shot in the wire last night. Major Hancock wants us to go out to the elephant grass and see whether we've got enemy troops nosing around out there."

Sappers hadn't been much of a problem at this camp, and it frightened Rick to think that trouble of that kind could start. But he disliked the idea of the patrol even more. He had little experience with elephant grass.

Most of what he knew had come from hearing men talk about it. The grass had an edge that could cut like a sword, and moving around in it was like walking in a maze, since it was usually higher than a man's head. In the grass, a man couldn't get a read on the sounds around him, and that was another problem. The jungle was scary, but a man could usually see; the grass was foreign territory to a long-range patrol soldier.

Rick put his letter away and stood up. "What do we take?" he asked.

"Not much," Woodward said. "We're not going to be out there overnight. Take your rucksack and a meal or two, and put in a claymore, just in case we have to set up a perimeter. Otherwise, just take water and M-16 ammo—and double up on grenades."

Rick understood. Shooting a rifle in the grass was almost pointless unless someone was right on top of the shooter, but a grenade could be lobbed toward the sound without giving away a man's own position.

Williams was swearing about elephant grass and extra patrols, but he began gathering up what he needed for his rucksack. Woodward said he would be back in fifteen minutes, and he left.

"I don't like the sound of this," Rick said.

"Chances are, we won't make contact," Kent told him. "I've been out there before and the biggest danger is just getting cut up by the grass. Wear gloves and try to keep the grass off your face."

The men applied their camo and organized their gear, then picked up their weapons from the supply sergeant. They followed Sergeant Woodward to a gate in the wire. A couple of guys on guard duty let the team out, and the men hiked across an open, sandy area and on into the grass.

Rick had walked through elephant grass a couple of times before, but only when he was heading into the jungle. He'd never spent a whole day in it. Sergeant Woodward told Kent to take the point and to move slowly. He whispered to the men, "Don't let that long grass flip back at the next man. Take it one step at a time and try to slip through without tramping everything down. Williams, you walk rear security and lift up that grass after we pass through."

"I've tried that before," Williams said. "It doesn't work."

"If you lift the best you can, it starts to straighten up before too long. We don't want to leave trails out here for the gooks to follow."

Rick was thinking that this patrol was insane. He couldn't see how they could find anyone in the grass, and he didn't like the thought of some NVA soldier picking up their trail.

For over an hour the men moved slowly. There was nothing to see, no point in being ready to shoot. But Rick felt uncomfortable, blinded. In spite of all his care with the grass, he had taken a couple of cuts across his cheek. The heat was coming on too. Rick was sweating through his fatigues and beginning to feel weak by the time the team finally took a break and drank some water. Williams used the chance to whisper to the sergeant, "Woody, what are we doing out here? There ain't nothing going on—or if there is, we won't find it."

The words had hardly left his mouth before Rick heard something. Everyone else did too; Rick could see it in their eyes. No one could move through the grass without making brushing sounds, and no question, something was moving out there. Gradually the sound got louder, and it was clear that this was no small unit. It had to be at least a platoon, maybe a company, working its way through the grass, probably in a line, and most likely heading toward the camp. Rick knew that sappers worked at night, so he wasn't sure about a troop movement like this. Maybe they were moving up to start blasting the camp with mortars and RPGs— Russian rocket-propelled grenade launchers.

Woody signaled with his hand for the men to sit tight, but no one needed to tell them. This was no time to make contact, not with four men against a large force. But Rick couldn't tell where the sound was coming from. For all he knew, the troops might stumble directly into their path. He waited, taking panting little breaths and holding still. To his relief, he realized that the soldiers were moving in a line just past them. Woody waited until their sounds became distant, and then he whispered to Williams, "Get TOC on the radio."

Once Williams had communication, he gave the handset to Sergeant Woodward. "Oh-one. Oh-one. Two-two here," he said. "Gooks moving to your wire. Alert camp. Over."

"Roger that alert, two-two. Give us a sitrep. Over."

"Moving to avoid contact, oh-one. Have gunships ready. Over."

"Get yourself clear, two-two. Give us a sitrep when you're ready. Over."

"Roger, oh-one. Out."

Woody gave the handset back to Williams, and then he whispered to the men, "We can't go back the way we came. If they crossed our trail, they could have an ambush set up. Preacher, take us a little farther out, away from the wire to the west, then head north. After the gunships do their thing, we'll make a wide arc back to the north end of the camp."

Kent slipped on his rucksack and stood. He checked his compass, then took his first careful steps. Rick followed, still in slack position.

Rick wondered what might be going on back toward the camp. He hoped the troops back there wouldn't take fire before the gunships could get up. The Cobras could give the NVA a workover. The only problem was, once the shooting started those enemy troops would be streaming back toward the west, and probably not in a line. If his team didn't get well out of the way, there was danger of contact. That wouldn't be so bad if the team was dealing with stragglers, but if a platoon was around them and a firefight broke out, anything could happen. The NVA might also be keeping another unit in reserve. The team could walk right into a sizable force if it got careless. Still, Kent would know what to do. He wouldn't get anxious and start moving too fast.

The men moved slowly, with the heat getting worse all the time and the tension adding to the rising temperature. Rick was starting to feel dizzy; he needed water. But Woody wasn't about to stop the team with a possible attack on their own camp imminent.

After a time Kent came to a stop. Rick could see what he was wondering about. He'd come across a trail where the grass was beaten down, even worn away. The trail had obviously been used plenty, and not just today. Kent waved for Woody to come up, and then he whispered, "What do you think? We could use this path to get north pretty fast, and then call in the gunships."

"That might be a good way to get ourselves ambushed," Woody said. "Besides, we've mined some of these trails out here ourselves. I was told to stay in the grass."

"I understand that. But we need to get the guns in the air right away."

Woody thought for a few seconds and then nodded.

"Okay. Let's use the trail and get a couple hundred meters to the north. Then we'll call in a sitrep and sit tight. But be careful. Watch for wires or any sign the ground has been disturbed."

Rick didn't like the sound of that. He never liked walking on a trail—not in the jungle and not here. All the same, he did like moving faster, and he did like the feeling that he was getting away from the destruction those Cobras would inflict. Kent was walking much faster now. After a few minutes Rick figured they'd covered a hundred meters and still had about that far to go. He could keep himself going that long.

But then the earth erupted.

Flying debris struck him in the face. He was thrown backward. At the same moment, he saw Kent's body flying up and sideways, cartwheeling off the path. Rick's face stung, and he was out of breath, but he didn't think he was wounded. After a few seconds, he struggled to his feet. By then Williams and Woodward had run past him and were pulling Kent back to the trail. He was moaning fiercely.

"You're okay, Preacher," Woodward was saying. "We'll get you out of here."

But Rick could see the truth. Kent's right foot was gone. Blood was gushing from the tattered stump. The left leg was bleeding too. Blood was seeping through his shredded fatigues all the way from his thigh to his boot. He had to have help, and he had to have it soon.

With both legs pumping blood, he could bleed to death.

"Lord," Rick heard Kent say, "please help me." He moaned again. The pain was obviously terrible.

"Williams, call in," Woodward said. "Get the gunships ready. Tell 'em we'll get Preacher north as fast as we can. We'll pop smoke here and again when we're far enough out for a medevac."

Suddenly Rick was focused. He had to get Kent to safety. Williams was trying to get a field dressing on the end of Kent's leg. Rick pulled the towel from his neck, reached under the leg, and cinched the towel tight, as a tourniquet.

"I'll get you to a slick," he told Kent. "I'll take care of you."

Woody turned to toss out a smoke grenade. At the same moment Rick grabbed Kent's arms and pulled him up and over his shoulder in a fireman's hold. "Let's go," he told the others, and he took off hard, heading north along the trail.

"No, no!" Woody was calling.

Rick slowed a little because he knew what Woody was thinking. There could be other mines ahead. But he didn't care. He wasn't going to let Kent die.

"You're going to get you *and* Preacher killed," Woody called, and that stopped him.

Woody caught up quickly. "I'll walk point. Williams, help Ward carry Preacher. Keep his legs higher than his head."

Rick lowered Kent, and Williams grabbed onto him. They walked with Kent in a basket hold, with his legs held high. Kent wasn't moaning now, wasn't praying, either; his eyes had gotten glassy. Rick wondered whether the tourniquet was doing the job.

Woody moved ahead at a good pace, watching the ground. Rick no longer felt the heat, or anything else. He could only think that they had to get Kent into a dustoff, where medics could get some blood into him.

The men made their way forward another fifty meters or so, not the intended hundred, and Woody stopped and crouched down. "Okay, Williams, turn those Cobras loose and get the medevac in the air. I'll pop another smoke."

It all happened fast. The Cobras came up like black dragons and they let loose a flood of fire, red tracers streaming into the elephant grass. Rick had no idea whether the gunners could see the NVA troops out there, but he knew that lots of them would be running back through the grass, heading west. He just hoped they didn't angle to the north. In a few minutes the medevac was calling in on the radio. "They want the smoke now," Williams said.

Woody threw out a yellow smoke grenade, and instantly Williams whispered, "Confirm. Yellow smoke. Over."

Rick saw the medevac rush low over the grass in front of them, then slow down, raise its nose, and descend. He heard the metallic sound of small-arms fire hitting the helicopter. The enemy was close, but he didn't care. He had to get Kent on board. Rick and Williams reached the dustoff before it touched down. Two medics pulled Kent on board and the helicopter seemed to jump into the air, still taking fire. In seconds it swooped away, and now Woody and Williams and Rick had to face their other problem. Where were the enemy troops? Rick formed a little perimeter with the other two men, then waited.

The chaos continued. The gunships were sweeping back and forth, working their way west with each pass, and their miniguns were firing in a constant roar.

Rick hoped the gunners were tearing up every gook who had sneaked into that grass. "Kill 'em!" he shouted.

"Shut up," Woody hissed.

But nothing was moving around them. The troops that had fired on the medevac were apparently more interested in distancing themselves from the Cobras than in making contact with Americans on the ground. After sitting tight for maybe twenty minutes, Woody moved the men out. They looped around to the camp and back inside the wire.

Rick went back to his tent. The other men in the platoon were gone, all out on alert because of the attack. Rick sat on his cot and shook. How could this have happened? Even a guy as good as Kent wasn't protected out there.

He wondered about Kent's family. They'd all be devastated. Rick was almost certain Kent would live, but he was messed up. Maybe he would lose both feet. How hard was that going to be?

Rick didn't want to think of himself. He tried not to. But he was alone now, and he had 260 days to go. Forever. He couldn't think how he was going to survive. "One day at a time," Kent had always said. Rick tried to breathe deep, to calm down. Things like this happened in war. But he kept seeing that gruesome leg, the torn red flesh, the broken white bone. He remembered how he'd felt the day Sparks had gone down. He wanted to feel that fury again. He needed it now. He tried to tell himself it was all the fault of those smelly little gooks who crept around in the grass, setting traps. But he knew the truth: The mine that had exploded was probably one of their own. There was really nothing to hate but the war itself, and that was like hating the world. Now Kent's legs were messed up, the same as Trang's. And so many more casualties would follow—legs and arms and heads and chests. Forever and ever people had been fighting. And for what? There would never be an end to it all. The dying was never going to stop.

CHAPTER 12

RICK TOOK A SHOWER, THEN LAY ON HIS COT. HIS STRENGTH WAS gone, but when the men from his platoon started coming back he ended up telling and retelling the story of what had happened out in the elephant grass. He didn't have the guts to tell them what he'd actually had on his mind while they were gone. So he told the story the way he thought they wanted to hear it, using their language, their way of thinking. "I'm going to get some gooks," he vowed to the men. "I'm going to kill all of 'em I can—and pay back for what they did to Preacher."

"That's right. That's what we gotta do," the men kept telling him.

But maybe they were going through the motions too. They didn't sound all that convincing. He heard the sorrow in Williams's voice when he said, "Preacher's legs were torn up real bad. One foot was gone, but I hope the doctors can save the other one." The tent got quiet after that.

Rick found himself wishing he had been the one to step on the mine. Kent hadn't deserved to get so messed up. But there was a deeper truth that Rick didn't want to think too much about. The fact was, he was almost jealous of Kent. He would probably trade a foot for the chance to get out of this place. He still had almost nine months to go. It was the end of May, and he wouldn't cycle out until February. The future had come to seem inevitable: Sooner or later, he'd get killed or shot up. Better to have it happen now, and better to have a foot blown off than to get a bullet through his head. If he had the guts, he'd do it to himself: aim his M-16 at his own foot and blow a hole through it. Other guys had done it; Rick had heard the stories. He could claim he was just cleaning his weapon. It wouldn't matter if anyone believed him.

But Rick knew he couldn't do it. He shut his eyes and tried to think.

In some ways Kent hadn't been good for him. The guy was always fighting himself, trying to think of the gooks as God's children, the same as him. That was fine for church, but it didn't work in a war. Rick couldn't afford to think that way.

"How you holding up, Ward?"

Rick opened his eyes. Williams had sat down on the cot that had been Kent's.

"I'm all right," Rick said. He took a breath. He didn't want Williams to hear any shakiness in his voice. "I'll be a lot better when we get back to the woods." He cursed and then added, "We all need to get us some payback, next time out."

"Yeah," Williams said, but not with any force. "That was rough out there, wasn't it?"

Rick was surprisingly moved by the question. He sat up and looked at Williams. "Yeah, it was," he said. "Do you think Kent will lose his other foot?"

"I don't know. I hope not. Either way, he's got some bad days ahead."

"But he's tough. He'll have a good attitude about it."

"Sure he will." Williams leaned forward, with his elbows on his knees. In a softer voice, he said, "I knew a guy who got shot up really bad. He took a lot of shrapnel in his chest and belly, and one hand was all broken up. He lived for a long time—like two months—and he was in bad pain the whole time. Then he died in surgery. If you ask me, that's the worst. I want to get my bullet right between the eyes. I don't want to feel a thing when it happens."

"Is that what you think—that it's going happen?"

Williams didn't answer for a time. "Sometimes I do," he finally said. "At first you think you'll never get hit, but after a while you start to feel like you're pushing your luck going out there over and over. We talk about being good at what we do, but we grab onto the tail of the tiger way too many times. You know what I'm saying?"

"Hey, I do."

Sergeant Pugmire came into the tent. He walked over to Rick's cot and said, "Ward, Williams, that was good work you men did out there. If those dinks had gotten in close without anyone knowing, they could have put a lot of fire in here before we got the gunships in the air. You saved lives today—maybe a lot of them."

"Thanks," Williams said.

"How bad's your buddy, Ward?"

The words were almost too tender. It wasn't something Rick expected from a guy like Pugmire. "Pretty bad," Rick said. "One foot was blown clear off." That was all Rick could say. He could feel his voice quavering again, and that infuriated him. He just had to stop acting like a baby.

Pugmire cursed the gooks, but then said, again in a way Rick never would have expected, "That's one of the worst things over here—when you make friends, and then your buddy gets tore up. After a while, you get so you don't want to make friends with nobody."

"The best friend I had over here got hit while we were out on a patrol together," Williams said. His voice lowered almost to a whisper. "It didn't look that bad, and we were pinned down, so I didn't try to get over to him. But he bled to death. If I'd known he was bleeding that bad, I would've crawled to him, no matter what. I think about that every day."

No one said anything for a long time. Finally Williams laughed weakly, and added, "He was a white guy, too. Growing up in East St. Louis, I didn't ever think I'd be buddies with a white guy."

"Hey, that's all right, Williams," Pugmire said, and he gave Williams a slap on the shoulder. "When we was growing up, we never thought we'd have to sleep in the same tent with a black guy. I figure the property value on my cot is down at least half with you so close by."

"Watch out, Pugmire. I'll get the brothers in here. We'll work you over sometime."

"Yeah, well, it'd take about nine of you."

Williams cursed Pugmire in mock anger, and then he stood up, laughing for real this time. And on the talk went. More men kept showing up, and a lot of them had good things to say to Rick. Some of them had beer, and Whiley brought a bottle for Rick. "Here you go, Killer," he said. Not many of the men had started calling him that, except for Whiley.

The beer was warm and tasted awful, but Rick drank it anyway. The talk turned back to wasting gooks—as many as possible. Rick was still feeling shaky inside, but he bragged as much as anyone and then he drank a second beer.

"Here's the thing about Preacher," J. D. told everyone. "He was too nice a guy to be a soldier. Guys like that don't make it over here."

But Whiley said, "I don't buy that, J. D. Ol' Preacher talked like he couldn't slap a mosquito without feeling bad about it, but I never worried when I was out there with him. He knew what he was doing, and I always knew, if I went down, he'd be the first guy to run through fire to help me out."

"Not you," J. D. said. "He thought you were *scum*."

"Well, that's because I am. So are you. But he still woulda done it for either one of us."

As night fell, some of the men built a bonfire outside, and most of the platoon went out and sat by it. There was more beer, more talk, more laughter, more stories.

Rick sat with them, but he wasn't saying much now. Too many things were running through his head, and the emptiness, the shakiness, was getting worse, not better. When he went inside that night, he got out his notebook.

Kent stepped on a mine today and got his foot blown off. I don't know where they took him or how bad he is. It seems weird to say, but Kent's the only friend I have anymore—anywhere in this world—and now he's gone. I know I've got to be a man about this. That's what I've been

telling myself all day, since it happened. But I
don't feel like a man. I wish I was a kid again,
hanging out with Renny and the guys back
home.

For the next few days Rick tried to find out what he
could about Kent, but no one knew anything. It
seemed as though men got medevacked out and then
disappeared. Rick asked about him so many times that
the company first sergeant finally said, "Look, Ward,
don't ask me again. I want to know what happened to
him as much as you, but the army ain't too worried
about whether we get word or not."

After that, Rick spent most of his time alone. He
wanted to be part of the talk around the tent, but he
couldn't find much to say. Williams checked on him
sometimes, but Williams was kind of a loner himself.
Much of the life around the camp had to do with
smoking dope or going to the EM Club to drink, and
Rick hated that place. It was filled up with prizes from
missions into the woods: AK-47s, Russian pistols, NVA
helmets, and even a skull someone had carried back
from the field. All the talk was full of beer and self-
importance. "That man always gets his kills," soldiers
would say, and it was considered great praise. Rick
wanted to belong, but too much was in his head, and
it was obvious that the other guys didn't quite believe
him when he tried to sound like them.

Three days after Kent had gone down, Rick pulled another patrol. What with the recent losses and some men finishing their tours and not being replaced, the numbers in the unit were down, so the platoon leader had had to reorganize some of the teams. Rick was still with Whiley and J. D., but a sergeant named Overman was their new team leader.

Rick didn't like the change. He had trusted Zeller. Overman was a bragger, like Whiley, but the word around the platoon was that he was getting too short. He was close to finishing his tour, so he was avoiding contact instead of looking for it. Rick didn't mind avoiding contact, but he'd also heard about soldiers getting nervous when they were short. Nervous soldiers made mistakes, and mistakes got people killed.

There was also another problem. A sergeant named Gartz was going to be ATL, and that wasn't sitting well with Whiley. Whiley had had more time in service than Gartz, more time in the jungle, and yet he'd never been promoted from corporal. Rick worried about going out with a team that wasn't unified.

On the morning of the mission, Rick waited at the helipad before sunup, his heart thudding in his chest. He was assigned to carry the radio, which wasn't as awkward and heavy as the thump gun, but it was a new responsibility. He was tense as the slick descended. But he did his job. The team inserted successfully, and after a minute or two of listening, he held the handset to his mouth and keyed the mike. "X-ray, X-ray," he whispered. "This is two-four. Commo check. Over."

"Two-four, this is X-ray," a deep voice came back. "Got you, Lima Charlie. Over."

"X-ray, this is two-four. Got you same, same." Then he had X-ray give him a count, one to ten and back, while he adjusted the sound on the radio. When he was finished, he nodded to Overman that they could move out. But Overman waited for a long time—too long, it seemed to Rick. He didn't know what Overman was thinking. Whiley and J. D. exchanged glances with Rick. Finally Overman motioned for the team to move out.

The plan was to work their way west, along a ridge, and then to hump several hills in their Area of Operation. If they could pick up fresh tracks or other signs of enemy presence, they would look for an ambush site. But other teams had been sent into this area recently, and the men had come back complaining that nothing was happening.

Rick wasn't sure what he wanted. He found himself hoping his team would make no contact. At the same time, he knew he needed to get a kill and not cry about it. He just wished that Overman would work the way Zeller had. Waiting at an LZ too long was dangerous. Maybe the rumors were right. Maybe Overman was being too careful.

The men worked their way silently through dense brush and then moved into the jungle. The trees made a single canopy, not the double or triple cover in much of the jungle, so light filtered through. But it was silent. There usually wasn't much sound in the jungle, but silence was frightening. It could mean that someone had been moving around ahead of them. Movement by troops would always quiet the birds, the monkeys, even the insects.

Rick hated the stink of the jungle. It smelled like death. It smelled like Sparks when he was down with his jaw shot off. Everything was always damp and rotting, and the humid air held the stench close.

The team worked their way forward for an hour or so at a time, taking ten-minute breaks. There was no water on the hillside, so the men were carrying lots of canteens and still using their water sparingly. By the time they finally ate, Rick was exhausted. As much as he feared contact, he'd come to understand why the men thrived on it. A four-day patrol with no contact meant three nights out and four hard days hiking with heavy rucksacks and constant tension. The tedious movement of small-unit troops, one careful step at a time, required infinite patience. When automatic fire opened up, the adrenaline would start pumping and they'd all be moving, firing. All the restraint was over. After the bullets stopped flying, there was exhilaration at being alive, and, at least for some guys, the excitement of making a kill. And after the kill, they'd get extracted. Charlie Rangers didn't stay to fight a platoon or company that might rush to the sound of the fire. As soon as an ambush or a fire-fight ended, slicks were on their way. The ideal patrol, all the men said, was to make contact the first day, get some kills, and get out.

But today the team hiked all day and then slept in a wagon-wheel formation, with their feet in the center of the circle. The claymores were out, but the jungle was eerie. Rick knew that toward morning the damp air would get cool and penetrating. He hated the long nights, especially waking to take his turn on alert. The enemy could be out there all around him; there was no way of knowing. And there were snakes in the jungle. Rick had seen them during the day. At night he would imagine them crawling over him. He'd heard stories about that. One man had awakened to find a bamboo viper, one of the deadliest of snakes, curled up against him like a friend. Rick didn't know anyone who had been killed by a snake, but men often came back with bad insect bites or with leeches all over them.

Rick didn't sleep well, but the night finally passed and the team hiked again the next day, up and over one hill in the morning and then another in the after-noon. When the men finally set up for a night perimeter, Rick found himself wondering about Overman. That morning Whiley, who was walking

170

point, had picked up a sound in the valley below. Whiley had wanted to move closer to the blue line and see what trails might be down there. Maybe they'd find evidence of troop movement. But Sergeant Overman told Whiley to move ahead as planned, away from the sound. Rick had seen Whiley take a long look at J. D., and he'd seen J. D. shake his head.

There was danger when the men didn't respect their TL, when team members weren't all thinking alike. Rick didn't like the feel of things.

Dark came early in the jungle as the sun angled low and no longer penetrated the density of the foliage. That meant the nights seemed twelve hours long. But Rick lay back and tried to relax. He wasn't a new guy now. He could handle this.

He wondered about Kent. Was he in a lot of pain? Was he on an airplane by now, flying home, or maybe already at some hospital in the States? Rick hoped that he'd see him again someday and find out how things had turned out. Rick also wondered how Trang and Vo Thi were doing. He needed to look out for them. No one else would do that now.

CHAPTER 13

RICK SLEPT BETTER THAT NIGHT, SO HE WAS STARTLED WHEN Sergeant Overman touched his shoulder to wake him.

"Whiley just heard something. We're all on alert," he said.

Rick reached carefully for his rifle and then rolled slowly off his back. After a time he thought he heard movement, but sound could carry a long way at night, and he had no idea how close the noise was. What seemed likely was that NVA troops had picked up some sign of the team's presence and were hunting for them.

But nothing happened. The men stayed awake until morning finally came and a dull light filled the jungle under the high canopy of teak and mahogany trees. They took turns eating their rations, and then Overman gathered them close and whispered, "I know we haven't made contact, but it looks like the gooks have a pretty good idea where we are. We're going to work our way to the ridge line above us, then call in slicks for an extraction."

"The CO won't buy that," Whiley said. "Not unless we've got more to go on than what we've heard so far."

"You let me worry about the CO. Ward, call in a sitrep. Tell 'em we've had movement around us all night. We're moving toward an extraction LZ."

"Sergeant," Whiley said, "we're out here to *kill* gooks, not run from them. We can—"

"That's enough, Whiley. Ward, call the relay team."

Rick whispered into the handset, "X-ray, X-ray, this is two-four. We've got movement outside our perimeter. Do you copy? Over."

"Roger that, two-four. Over," came the answer.

"X-ray, we're moving to the ridge for extraction. Over."

"Roger. Out."

Rick knew that wasn't necessarily the end of the matter. The relay team would pass on the information, but the CO might tell Overman to continue the mission—unless, of course, the team made contact with the enemy.

Rick watched Whiley, who was clearly disgusted. He was looking at the other men, communicating with his eyes that he didn't think much of Overman's decision. But Rick knew what a team leader had to consider. LRP teams were too small to take on larger units. They were only successful when they had surprise working for them. When a Charlie Ranger team found enemy soldiers moving in the jungle, the goal was to ambush them and kill them. If it was the team that was being hunted, a firefight could bring a whole platoon in against them. Overman was right to be careful.

Overman had the men saddle up, and once they had their rucks on, he waved his arm to signal that it was time to move out. Whiley walked point again, and he was precise in placing one foot at a time, moving wait-a-minute vines or limbs, not trying to push through them, and all the while watching ahead, left, right, like a machine. The other men moved with the same care, and they stayed in fairly dense foliage, not taking a chance with trails. The climb seemed endless and made Rick nervous. A couple of times he thought he heard movement again, and he knew Whiley was picking up on something because he was taking long stops to listen.

Rick watched his step, glancing ahead to keep pace with Whiley. When he saw Whiley crouch, Rick hunched down too. He clicked the selector switch on his M-16 to automatic, then waited and scanned the foliage. Suddenly there was a muzzle flash and a blast of fire from two o'clock, ahead of them. At the same time, Whiley fired on full automatic, sending red tracers careening through the vegetation. There was silence after that. Rick crouched lower. He was ready to move, if that's what he had to do. But time kept passing and nothing happened. Maybe there had been only one man out there and Whiley had killed him.

From behind him, Rick heard Overman whisper, "Ward, call in the contact."

Rick already had the handset in his hand. "X-ray, this is two-four. Contact. Do you copy? Over."

"Roger the contact, two-four. Over."

"Okay, men, let's fall back," Sergeant Overman said. "Keep the noise down, but let's get down this hill to the blue line and across. We've got an E and E site on the other side of the stream."

Whiley was walking backward, keeping low. "Just a minute," he whispered. The men had pulled into a tighter perimeter. As Whiley reached them, he said, "This looks like an ambush to me. I think they fired on us just to send us down the hill. They'll be waiting for us below, maybe at the blue line."

"You don't know that," Overman said. "We've gotta get out of here, and that's where our LZ is set up."

"Sergeant, someone fired on us and then fell back fast. I didn't kill him. That's a sure sign they didn't want to fight us up here. They just want to get us running into their main force. We could move around the hill, to the east, then head for the ridge."

"All that does is keep us in the jungle longer, and we've probably got gooks coming from all directions now. Whiley, take the point, and let's get to the stream as fast as we can without a lot of noise. Ward, call it in."

Rick watched Whiley. Whiley had been ready to

come back with another argument, but then he took a big breath and accepted the order. Rick didn't know who was right, but he didn't like the way Whiley was looking. No one had a better instinct about what the North Vietnamese troops were thinking than Whiley.

Rick radioed X-ray again, and then down the hill they went, moving faster than before, making some noise, but not giving up sound discipline altogether. They covered a distance in fifteen minutes that had taken them an hour before. As Whiley approached the bottom of the valley, he slowed things down, and when he spotted a wide well-used trail, he crouched and watched to check it out.

Overman moved up and knelt next to him. Rick could see that they were whispering, and he knew what they were trying to decide. Was it okay to cross the trail and wade across the river? There wasn't any cover once they left the vegetation they were hiding in now.

When they stopped talking, Whiley moved out, alone. He stepped carefully across the trail and into the creek. The water ran over his boots but wasn't deep, and the LZ wasn't far beyond. Rick was beginning to feel that they would get out all right. Then he heard the rattling crack of automatic fire again. Whiley slumped into the water, facedown.

Rick dropped to one knee and looked frantically around to see where the fire had come from. But Overman was calling, "Fall back. Fall back."

That made no sense. Rick knew it instantly. And Gartz knew it too. "No!" Gartz said, and then scuttled forward and crouched next to Overman. "Sergeant, they've got us from both sides. We can't fall back. Our only hope is to get across that river."

Overman seemed paralyzed. He did nothing, said nothing, but Gartz turned and whispered, "Ward, call in gunships. Tell 'em to rake the blue line, up and down. Then we'll cross."

Rick made the call. By then the CO had gotten into the air in a Bird Dog airplane. He called in his response directly. "Two-four, this is Bird Dog. Roger the gunships. Two mikes."

Two minutes. But what about Whiley? He was still in the water, which was flowing pink with his blood. If he was alive and didn't drown, the Cobras would get him. Someone had to pull him out of there.

Rick moved closer to Overman and Gartz. "What about Whiley?" he asked.

"There's nothing we can do about him right now," Overman said with force—as though he wanted to let everyone know he was back in charge. "We gotta let the guns do their work before we can go out there."

Rick shook his head. "No way, Sarge. That's not right."

"Step back," Overman insisted. "Be ready with that radio."

But Rick was pulling off his rucksack. "Whiley

would never leave *you* out there, Sarge," he said. "Here's the radio. I'm going to get him."

"No!"

Rick stepped around Overman and jumped onto the trail. He swung his weapon right and left, blasting the foliage, and then he ran to the river. He could see that Whiley was struggling to keep his head above the water. He was still alive. Rick fired again, up the stream and then down, before he slung his rifle over his shoulder and jumped into the water. He grabbed Whiley and turned him over. He reached under his arms and hoisted him as best he could. Stumbling and struggling, walking backward, Rick managed to pull Whiley onto the opposite bank. Whiley was moaning, and Rick could hear the gurgling, bubbling sound as his chest wound sucked air. It sounded bad.

Rick got a better grip and lifted Whiley higher, struggling backward again. He made good headway for ten yards or so. He heard bullets flying by, but he paid no attention. Then something hit him in the side, like a fist slamming into his ribs. He went down, hard, but he was up again instantly, and he grabbed Whiley again. Pain seared through his side and his chest, but he moved Whiley several more yards before his left leg was hurled out from under him. He tried to fight his way back up to his feet, but his leg gave way. Still, he grabbed Whiley by his fatigues and used his good leg to push backward. He was getting almost nowhere, and he was running out of strength, but he kept scrabbling, pulling. He had to get Whiley, and himself, out of the way of those gunships.

Then he heard a roar and felt the earth shake. The Cobras had reached the river. They were tearing everything up, firing just over him. Rick pushed again with his right leg, grabbed at the earth with his hand, and pulled, managing to move them another couple of yards away. He hoped the pilots could see him.

He breathed hard, felt the pain in his ribs, and then he pulled again. Maybe they were safe. The side gunners should be able to see the two of them on the ground, out there in a clearing. But now he had to do something to help Whiley. He could hear how ragged Whiley's breathing was. Rick felt in his pockets, found a field dressing, and tore Whiley's fatigues open. The roar of fire from the gunships engulfed him. Rick wanted desperately to get farther away, but he didn't think he had the strength to pull again.

Rick pressed the field dressing to the wound on the left side of Whiley's chest, but he wasn't sure that would help. He didn't know exactly what he should do and he couldn't think clearly now. His vision was blurring. He was all pain, everywhere—his body and legs, his head.

Suddenly the firing stopped. Rick looked toward the river and he saw three men from his team break out of their cover and charge across. J. D. ran hardest and reached Rick and Whiley first. He dropped down next to them.

"We gotta get him bandaged better than that," Rick said.

"No," J. D. said, "the slick is coming in. Help me get him on board."

J. D. jumped up and grabbed Whiley by one arm. Rick fought his way onto one foot, and was partway up before he knew without hearing them that bullets were flying again. He glanced toward J. D. just as the man's head exploded. Blood and brain flew in a red crescent, and J. D. stood still for a moment, most of his head gone. Then he crumpled to the ground.

Gartz was next to Rick by then, firing his weapon back toward the river. "Get Whiley!" he screamed.

Rick felt a surge of adrenaline. He got up again, got his bad leg under him this time, and grabbed Whiley under the arms. He lurched backward, pulling hard, but his leg crumpled beneath him. Gartz was still firing, and Rick worked his way up again, pulled again. And then, finally, Overman was next to him, helping. But Rick couldn't keep up. He went down again. Gartz moved back, grabbed Whiley, and he and Overman dragged him away. Rick began to pull himself along the ground, pushing with one leg, pulling with his hands in the grass. He could hear the slick. He didn't have far to go, but he couldn't see now, couldn't make sense of anything.

He didn't know that he'd blacked out until he felt a hard jerk on his arms, and pain shot through his side. He was sliding across the grass on his back, the pain almost more than he could stand, but then he was hoisted and pulled by more hands, and he felt his head crack against the metal floor of the helicopter.

As the slick lifted, Rick felt the pull on his body. The pain was all through him now. Gartz was ripping his shirt open. Rick heard him curse when he looked at the wound. That scared Rick, but he was more worried about something else.

"Whiley?" Rick asked.

"What did you say?"

It was hard to speak. "Whiley?"

"I don't know. But stay with me, you hear? We'll get you patched up. We're only ten mikes out, and we're going to get this bleeding stopped."

Rick tried to speak again. "Leg."

Gartz looked at Rick's leg and cursed again. "That's all right. We'll get that stopped too. And we've got morphine. You're okay."

Rick had heard soldiers tell dying soldiers they were all right. Was he dying? And what about Whiley? Was he dead already? Then he felt the jab in his hip, and a wave of calm passed through him, the pain not leaving, but feeling distant. He struggled to keep his eyes open, but he was drifting and he couldn't hold on to the light.

CHAPTER 14

EVERYTHING WAS BLURRY. BUT RICK REMEMBERED. HE'D BEEN AWAKE before, here in this room. There was a nurse somewhere; he knew that. She'd tried to wake him and he'd tried to tell her his name. She was a big woman with wide shoulders, but she'd spoken in a soft voice; she'd smiled at him and patted his hair, as though he were a child.

Rick looked for her now, but the bed was pulling on him, holding his head in place. He drifted again until he heard her voice. "Hey, sleepyhead, are you going to wake up now?"

Rick opened his eyes. She wasn't as big as he'd thought. She had pretty lips, full, with no lipstick.

"Do you remember where you are?"

He tried to answer, but his throat was clogged. He coughed a little and said, "Hospital."

"That's easy. Anyone could guess that. But what hospital?"

He didn't know.

"Don't you remember?"

"No."

"Hey, we're having a conversation. That's good. This is the 93rd Evac hospital, at Long Binh. I'm Lieutenant Griggs. Do you remember that now?"

"Yes."

"Okay, then, say it to me."

It was like asking him to lift something heavy. Still, he tried to say it.

"Hey, that's not too bad. I'm not giving you a hard time. I just want you to come back to the world of the living. You lost a lot of blood. You looked like a dead man when they brought you in."

"What about Whiley?"

She shook her head. "I couldn't understand you. Try that again."

Rick breathed, long and slow. He tried to turn his head so he could see her better, but she'd stepped away. He was in a little room with white walls, and he remembered something else. He had had surgery. She'd told him before. The bullet had slashed through his intestines, but a doctor had sewn up the holes. He would be all right.

"Is Whiley here?"

"Who's Whiley?"

Rick tried to think of the answer. Time passed, she asked again, and then he was able to say, "Corporal Green."

"Is he your friend?"

"Yes."

"This is a big place. I don't know whether he was brought here or not. I'll find out." She touched his hair again. "It's okay to sleep some more now. If you need me, I won't be far away."

She left and Rick drifted again. He didn't think that he'd slept, and yet she was back in what seemed like seconds. "He's here, but he's in a lot worse shape than you are. He's already had some major surgery. They're going to get him stabilized and then he'll need at least one more operation. He'll probably go back to the States for that."

But he was alive. Rick was glad. He thought of J. D. and shuddered. He didn't want to remember how he'd died.

For the next couple of days Rick didn't know day from night, or how long he slept. But Lieutenant Griggs and the other nurses on the shift kept him talking when they could, and through the cloud of medicine he was taking, he pieced together an idea of his future. He'd been patched up pretty well, and chances were he wouldn't need any more surgery. He'd lost a big hunk out of the calf of his leg, but the bones weren't broken. He'd stay at the hospital until he was well enough to travel back to the States, and then he would put in some more time back there. A doctor told Rick that he'd be getting out of the army once he'd recovered. The wound in his left side had pierced his intestines and torn up his spleen, which had been removed. It might be many months before Rick was entirely back to normal.

It was June now. Nearly a year had passed since he'd enlisted, but it felt like decades. The boy who had walked into the recruiting office the year before was long gone. He tried to think what he wanted to do now, what lay ahead for him, but he found the whole idea hard to imagine: being home, going on with life.

Every day Rick asked about Whiley. He hoped that he could see him at some point. He'd heard Whiley was heavily sedated and couldn't talk yet.

Meanwhile Rick had finally received a letter from Kent, who was in an army hospital in Oakland, California. Kent was going be fitted for a prosthetic leg once his stump had healed enough, and he wrote that he didn't think he'd have a hard time learning to use it.

> I'm a lot better off than most of the guys I see every day. I've only got the one leg gone, below the knee, which is hardly even a chal- lenge, from what they tell me. The other leg is messed up, but it's going to work okay. So I don't feel too sorry for myself. I guess there will be some things I can't do, but not too many. I'm just glad you guys got me out of there. The doc back in Nam told me that

I lost so much blood, I came within a minute or two of dying.

I've heard how you and Zeller and Williams took a big chance to get me medevacked, and I know the pilot took fire coming in. I'll owe you forever, Rick. I hope everything goes all right for you now. And I hope we can keep in touch. When you get out of the army, come up to Idaho and we can go for a hike in the woods. I promise, we won't do any hunting.

Kent also had added a P.S.: "Say hello to Trang and Vo Thi for me. The money in the envelope is for them." He had sent twenty dollars.

All of Rick's gear had been sent to him from camp. He had his notebook back. After a time he tried to sort out what he was feeling.

I heard from Kent today. He sounded pretty good. He figures he'll be able to get around all right with a wooden leg. I'm glad he's going to be all right, but I wish he hadn't thanked me. We barely got him out in time. I've been thinking, I never should have stopped when Sergeant Woodward told me to. If I'd been the one hit, Kent would have kept right on running, no matter what. If Kent had died, I don't know how I could live with myself now.

At least I didn't let Whiley die. And when I got hit, Gartz and Overman got me on the slick even though they could have been shot too. I've been thinking about that all the time lately— how soldiers do things like that. I'm not that close to most of the guys in my platoon, but back in the world people don't die for each other, and out here they do. J. D. died for Whiley. I don't know a lot of good things to tell anyone about J. D., and yet, when I try to compare my friends in Long Beach, I don't think any of them would put their lives on the line for me. I'm relieved to get out of Vietnam, but I know I'll never experience anything like this again. I doubt I'll ever feel so close to anyone, even if it's someone I like a lot better.

I wish I didn't have to keep seeing, in my mind, what happened to J. D.'s head when the bullet hit him. Kent thinks that a spirit is inside a body. I hope he's right. I hope J. D.'s not just roadkill.

I keep wondering now what life is for, or what it means. Sometimes I thought about that back home, and Judy and I talked about it some. But when you get shot and don't die, you wonder why some guys get wasted over here and some guys go home. I've got to decide what I'm going to do with my life. It seems like I ought to

187

*do something worthwhile. For a long time I
didn't think I'd learned anything from being in
Nam, but maybe I have. If a guy's in the river,
bleeding, you pull him out, even if it costs you
something. Not everyone back home under-
stands that. Not even everyone over here under-
stands it. But it's what I want to remember
when I get back. There are people facedown in
rivers back in the world, too.*

Rick was in the evac hospital in Long Binh for four
weeks. By then he was up walking every day and was
doing pretty well. He talked to Whiley a couple of
times, but Whiley was still on a lot of painkillers and
not making much sense.

When Rick found out he was being flown back to the
States, he asked for permission to catch a ride back to
Phan Thiet to say good-bye to his platoon. But the main
thing was, he needed to see Trang and Vo Thi. He wanted
to take Kent's money to them, but he also wanted to be
sure they were doing all right before he left the country.

"I can't send you back down there," the doctor told
him. "But I can release you in a few days, instead of
today, and I can look the other way if you manage to
catch a ride down there with a medevac team or
someone like that." Phan Thiet was not far away, so
Rick was sure he could find a flight. He thanked the
doctor and asked around about transportation. It

looked as if he could get a flight without a problem. But he couldn't leave without saying good-bye to Whiley.

Whiley was in a ward with five other guys, but his bed was the first one, just inside the door. Rick approached the bed slowly. Whiley was asleep.

"Hey, corporal, saddle up," Rick whispered.

Whiley's eyes came open. "Hey," he said.

"Do you know what I'm saying, or are they still shooting you up with too much dope?"

"There's nothing but good Texas blood in my veins, man," Whiley said, and he grinned. "But I could use a cold beer right now if you can get me one."

"It would run right back out. You're full of holes."

"Not now. They put patches on everything—just like fixin' an inner tube."

Rick smiled and nodded. "That's good," he said. And then, seriously, "I'm getting out of here, Whiley. I'm flying down to see all the Charlie Rangers one last time, and then they're shipping me home."

"Good for you, man. The guys in the platoon will give you a hard time, but it's all just talk. You earned this trip."

"I was lucky. The bullet that got me was over to the side. It didn't hit as much stuff as the one that got you."

Whiley looked at Rick for a long time, and then he looked away. When he spoke, his voice was strained. "I was dying, Ward. I was trying to keep my head up, but I was about finished. Then you jumped in there and pulled me out. I'll never forget that as long as I live. You took a couple of bullets for me. There ain't nothing any better in this world a guy can do for somebody else."

"J. D. took one in the head. I guess that's more."

"Was it in his head?" Whiley looked back at Rick.

"Yeah. One shot. He was dead on the spot."

"That's good. I've been wondering. I didn't want to find out he suffered." Whiley looked at the wall again. "So how do I live with that?" he asked.

"You would've done it for him. That's how it works."

"I know. But I don't like it this way. I'd rather I'd gone down and he'd made it home. He had more to go back to."

"We don't get to choose, do we?"

"No."

Whiley was still looking at the wall, and Rick felt uncomfortable. A nurse was approaching them—a pretty Vietnamese woman.

"That's good for you, talking," she said. "Is this your friend, Whiley?" She pronounced it "wy-*lee*."

"Yeah, this is my friend. The one who pulled me out of the river. Without him I'd be dead and roasting in hell, where I belong."

"No, no. Not hell. You good man."

Whiley was clearly embarrassed. "She doesn't know me," he said, and Rick could tell that he meant it.

"I know you very well. I see your bottom every day."

Whiley laughed and then he said, with surprising affection, "Ward, this is Lien. Her name means Lotus, like the flower. She takes good care of me. And I was pretty rough on her at first."

Rick nodded. "Nice to meet you," he said.

She smiled. "Yes. Very happy." And then she walked away.

"Ward, tell everyone hello for me, okay? I'm glad I'm going home, but I'm going to miss those guys. They're the only friends I have anymore."

"Yeah. I've been thinking the same thing." Rick tried to laugh. "I'll tell everyone you're down here drinking beer and sitting in the sun."

"I don't care what you say about me, but tell 'em that I'm sorry I won't be able to get down there, and . . . you know . . . that I'll be thinking about them and everything. You know how to say stuff like that better than I can."

"Okay."

Rick reached his hand out. Whiley shook it and actually held on for a moment, and then he said, "Ward, me and J. D. were tough on you. But it's just what everyone does to new guys. And then . . . you started hanging around with Preacher."

"I know."

"You and Richards, you were a couple of . . . I don't know what to call you."

"Bleeding hearts."

"No. I don't know." Whiley looked at Rick but didn't meet his eyes. He seemed to be searching for something he wanted to say. "Look," he finally said, "I've got some money in this drawer right here. Take out two twenties—no, three—and take them with you. You're going to see that taxi driver, aren't you?"

"Yeah."

"Give it to him, okay? It ain't nothing I'd do, but it's for you and Preacher. And one for Lien."

"Okay." Rick opened the drawer and got the money, but he didn't say anything else. He didn't mind expressing his appreciation, but he didn't want to show his emotion, and there had been more of that in Whiley's voice than either one of them was comfortable with. So Rick tucked the bills into his pocket and shook Whiley's hand one more time.

"Look me up if you ever get to Lubbock," Whiley said.

"Okay." The strange thing was, Rick knew it would never happen. Back in the States everything would be different, but here, right now, Rick felt something too big for him to deal with. He wasn't sure he liked Whiley all that much, but he loved him. It was something he would probably never try to express to anyone—not even to Whiley—but it was true.

Rick caught his ride to Phan Thiet. He didn't get in until late in the afternoon, and he was tired after being up for so long. He was really dragging by the time he got to his old tent. Most of the Charlie Rangers were in that night, since they were going out to the jungle on a patrol the next morning. There were a few new guys, but Rick knew everyone else. The men gave him the usual razzing, telling him he hadn't taken much of a hit. But Rick could feel the change in their attitudes. He knew what the men really thought of him. Williams introduced him to a new guy by saying, "This is the man we told you about. He jumped into a river and pulled Whiley Green out. He took two bullets doing it, but he saved Whiley's life."

No one joked about that.

"It won't be the same around here without you and J. D. and Whiley," Williams told Rick. It was a strange combination of names, but Rick knew it wasn't said with irony.

"Preacher is doing all right," Rick told him.

"Yeah, we heard. He's probably organizing a movement to send help to all the wounded civilians."

"Yeah. Wouldn't surprise me." Rick looked around and then raised his voice so everyone could hear. "Say, listen. That reminds me. Whiley gave me some money to give to Trang Hoa, that taxi driver who got beat up so bad. He gave me sixty dollars. Preacher sent some too. Does anyone else want to chip in?"

There was silence for a time, and Rick knew what everyone was thinking. *Whiley* had chipped in to help a gook? But they must have been thinking about Preacher, too. The men reached into their pockets, and most of them had something to give.

CHAPTER 15

RICK FOUND AN UNOCCUPIED COT AND LAY DOWN IN HIS CLOTHES.
He didn't wake up until the next morning. The temperature had cooled enough to be almost comfortable by then. He listened to the snores and noticed the sour smell in the tent in a way he hadn't since he'd first arrived, almost four months before. He was surprised at the nostalgia he felt.

Most of the men piled out early. They had to be ready to go at 0600. Rick felt the nervousness in the tent as they packed up and applied camo to their faces, then headed out to pick up their weapons. He thought of walking to the helipad, just to see them off, but he knew he'd be out of place there. A lot of the men loved that moment when a slick lifted for a mission, but Rick had never gotten to that point. Even the memory closed off his throat. He had no desire to relive any of that.

He said good-bye to his friends again and then walked to the mess tent, where he took his time having breakfast. After, he walked out the camp gate and caught a taxi into town. When he knocked on Trang's door, he worried that it was still too early. But Vo Thi appeared, and her eyes widened at the sight of him. "Rick," she said, making the syllable seem shorter than when an American said it. She bowed her head a little and stepped back to ask him in. Then she called to Trang. Rick heard his name again amid the Vietnamese words she was saying.

Trang soon appeared from his bedroom, walking with a makeshift crutch under his arm and looking much better than when Rick had seen him last.

"Happy to see you!" Trang said, but he obviously noticed the change in Rick. "You okay?"

"I got shot. Right here." Rick pointed to his side. "And in my leg, like you."

Trang translated for Vo Thi, and Rick saw her look of concern. "I'm going home, Trang. That's the best part. I'm getting better, and I'm getting out of the army."

"This very good." Again he translated, and Vo Thi seemed happy for Rick. She nodded and smiled.

"Trang, you need to know too, Kent stepped on a land mine. He's back in America, and he's doing all right, but he lost his foot."

Trang looked shattered. When he told Vo Thi, tears filled her eyes.

"He has a good attitude about it. You know Kent."

Rick knew that Trang hadn't understood that. But Rick was talking mostly to himself anyway. And he was fighting not to feel too much. Vo Thi's beautiful dark eyes, her tears, were more than he could handle. He loved her gentleness. Would he ever have someone like her in his life?

"Are you getting better, Trang?"

"Yes, yes. Not too long, I drive taxi again."

Rick wondered if that was really true. Trang still couldn't put much weight on his bad leg. "Some of the men wanted to give you help. They sent this to you." He reached into his pocket and pulled out the bills. It was a big wad of cash, and Trang and Vo Thi looked shocked.

"No, no. Is too much," Trang said.

"If it's too much, help some other people. But I won't be back, and this has to last you until you can work again."

Trang held the money in the palms of both hands and stared at it. "This can help many people. Many people *need* this help," he said.

"I know. I'm sorry, Trang. I'm sorry for what's happened to your country." Rick stared across the room and fought to control his emotion again. "I think America has a good heart. I really do. We wanted to help your people. I'm sorry for the damage we've done instead."

This again was mostly for himself. He wasn't sure that Trang understood entirely. But Rick was thinking of all the refugees, all the destroyed villages and rice paddies, all the defoliated forests, all the death. He really wanted to believe, had to believe, that his country had set out to do something good, no matter what a mess this had all turned out to be. But the thought of it all, the muddle of it all, struck Rick as never before. He'd fought his tears as long as he could, and now he couldn't stop them. It was then that Vo Thi stepped to him and held him in her arms like a mother. Trang joined them and wrapped his arms around both of them. And Rick cried—cried harder than he had since the night before he'd left his home in California. He knew he would carry the ache and regret of this time in Vietnam forever. He was lucky. He was going home, but the war needed to end and the world needed to heal. And though it was probably stupid to hope for such a thing, somehow people had to stop doing this to each other.

He knew he couldn't leave them like this; he had to get himself back in control. "I'm sorry," he told them again. "I really am. I hope your lives will be better now."

"We hope for you, good friend," Trang told him. "Bless you. And bless Kent. We never forget you."

Rick caught another taxi back to camp. He rested that day. He caught a ride back to Long Binh on the following morning. Then he caught the "freedom bird" that took him home. He spent a couple more weeks at the Greater Los Angeles Veterans Hospital, in West Los Angeles, before he was released. He would still be checking back at the hospital for a few months, but once he was considered recovered, he would be discharged from the army.

Rick's parents visited him at the hospital a couple of times that summer of 1970, and then they picked him up on the morning he was released. On the drive back to Long Beach, he kept looking around, wondering why he had never been impressed by all this before: the bright buildings, the wide freeways, the speed of everything. He knew there were lots of poor people in the area, but the poverty in America looked like prosperity in Vietnam, and the nice neighborhoods were filled with palaces by Vietnamese standards.

His dad drove and his mom asked questions—the same questions she had asked when she had visited him before. She wanted to know about Rick's condition, his emotions. But Rick didn't want her to know. He'd never tell her what he had seen.

Dad finally asked, "So what's it like, sneaking around out there in the jungle the way you guys did?"

Rick was surprised at his own reaction. The question seemed stupid. Did his dad really think he could tell him? But he wanted to make a better start with his father, see whether they couldn't find some common ground.

"It's . . . pretty miserable in the jungle. You know, hot and sticky."

"How did you get shot?"

"We got caught in an ambush. We were trying to get to our helicopter so we could get extracted—you know, flown out." Rick stopped. He had no idea how to explain the whole thing. He wasn't going to try.

"The letter we got said you were helping another man. Your platoon leader said you saved his life."

"That's what we always did—all of us. If someone went down, the others helped him get back to the slick—you know, the helicopter."

"Maybe so. But they gave you a medal. That tells me you showed some bravery."

Rick had gotten word while he was in the hospital that he was getting a Silver Star. He hadn't thought much about that. Most of the men in Charlie Rangers laughed about medals. They all deserved them, so whether a guy got one or not seemed mostly political.

"Who was this guy whose life you saved?" his dad asked.

"His name is Whiley Green. He's from Texas. But it wasn't like they made it sound. I just . . . I mean, I helped him, and some other guys did too, and then they had to help me, because I was down. It's . . . I don't know, Dad . . . I don't know how to explain it to you."

"Well, I'm proud of you."

"Thanks." Rick was tempted to ask his father, "Are

you also proud of me for the guys I killed over there?" But he couldn't get into something like that and he knew it, so he said only, "Dad, I just want to forget all that stuff right now."

Mom understood, and she began to tell him about his friends, what little she knew, but it was all a foreign language to Rick. Most of his friends were going to junior college, and it sounded like they were still partying a lot. It seemed to him that half the world was on fire and the people who lived in the other half were getting out their marshmallows and sticks as though they had found a nice campfire.

Rick spent a lot of time at home for the next couple of weeks. He went to the vet hospital for his first follow-up, and he went for a few long drives by himself, but he didn't try to see his friends. Gradually word got out that he was back, and some of them called him, but they were like his dad. Flipper wanted to know whether he'd killed anyone. Rick wouldn't tell him, and things soon got awkward. Renny called too, and after a frustrating conversation, he finally said, "Are you all right, Rick? You sound like you've changed a lot."

"Yeah, well, you sound pretty much the same," Rick told him. Rick was sorry for his sarcasm, but he didn't mind that he didn't hear from Renny again.

But Rick did want to talk to someone. He wasn't sure what he wanted to say, but he was nervous just sitting around. There were things he needed to sort out, and he wasn't sure how to do that. He was having trouble concentrating. He tried to watch television, tried to read, tried to rest, tried to write, but nothing kept his attention very long. He would get up and pace, walk outside, come back in, borrow his mom's car, drive a few blocks, and then turn around and drive back. But the worst was trying to sleep. Dreams came every night, not always dreams of combat, but images—little vignettes—that took him back. More often than not he was hiding, and something was close by, looking for him. Suddenly the sounds and colors would crash through his head and he'd be out of breath, reaching for his M-16, sometimes screaming. Once he was walking down the hall by his bedroom while his dad was watching television in the living room. There was gunfire on TV and suddenly Rick was on the floor in the hall, breathing in high-pitched little grunts, trying to get up but unable to do it.

Roxie knew he wasn't doing well. She sensed it more than her parents. She told Rick she'd heard him yelling at night sometimes. He didn't want to say too much; he only admitted that he was having "stupid dreams."

"Soldiers, after they come back, they have dreams like that a lot of times," he told her.

"I have dreams about Dad screaming and telling me he's going to beat me up," she said.

"He didn't do that, did he?"

"No. But he told Mom he was going to divorce her. He said that a hundred times while you were gone. Mom just tries to calm things down, and that only makes him madder."

Rick had no idea what to do about that. He wanted Roxie to grow up and get out, and he wanted Mom to stand up for herself. He tried to talk to her about doing that, but she told him things were fine now. Dad had lost his temper a while back, and that had been bad, but things had been a lot better since then. His mother had managed to get by with her life the way it was for a long time, and he figured she'd keep doing that. It all made about as much sense to Rick as the war did. There were things in this world that just shouldn't happen, and yet they did.

What Rick really needed to do was move ahead with his own life, but his heart would start to race every time he tried to come up with a plan. Life was looking a lot longer than those 365 days he'd worried so much about, and he didn't have anyone telling him when his next patrol would go out.

He'd heard that Judy was home for the summer. So on an impulse he drove to her house one evening and simply showed up on her porch. Her mom came to the door and seemed not to know him for a moment. "Rick, I hardly recognized you. Are you all right?"

"Yeah, I'm all right. I got wounded in Vietnam, but I'm pretty much okay now."

"You've lost a lot of weight. Maybe *I* need to get wounded." She tried to laugh, but when Rick didn't smile, she was obviously embarrassed. "I'll get Judy."

Rick sat in Judy's living room, the same room where he'd seen her the last time they'd said good-bye. It seemed years ago now. When Judy appeared, she looked good—less the hippie, and maybe less intense. She was wearing a simple little sundress, with a short skirt and sunflowers in the fabric.

"Rick, how are you?" she said, but now she was seeing what her mother had seen, and her eyes were showing the same surprise.

"I'm okay. I've lost some weight, but . . ." He couldn't think what to tell her.

"Mom says you got shot."

"Yeah. But you know, it wasn't too bad."

"Where's your wound?"

"In my side, over here. I had to have surgery, but it worked out fine. And I got hit in the leg, too. In my calf." He pointed to his left leg.

Judy's face softened. "This *stupid* war!" she said. "I hate it."

Rick hated the war too, but he doubted they thought the same way about it. "It's a bad situation," was all he could think to say.

She hesitated, then walked toward him. "Can I— can I give you a hug? I feel so bad you got hurt."

"Sure." He stood, and she put her arms around him.

He wasn't prepared for the emotion he felt. When she stepped back, she looked at his eyes, and she was obviously surprised by what she saw there. She hugged him again and said, "Are you going through a hard time?"

He shrugged. He didn't want to answer the question. He sat down again on the upholstered chair behind him. She turned a matching chair and sat down, so they were facing each other.

"You can tell me. Rick, what's happening to you?"

"I'm not sure." He clasped his hands together in his lap and looked down at them. "I'm nervous, for one thing. It's just hard to get back into things. I've got to get my strength back a little more before I can get a job or go to school, so for now, I don't quite know what to do with myself."

"How bad is it over there, Rick?"

"It's . . . uh . . . ," His hands lifted, palms up. "I don't know how to describe it."

Judy nodded. "You don't have to say anything. I can see what it's done to you. It's ruined so many lives and it hasn't accomplished anything. Nixon is such a liar! He promised to bring the troops home and now he's taking forever to do it."

Rick shifted in his chair. "It's not going to work, anyway. Once our troops come home, the North Vietnamese will overrun the south."

She pounced on the words. "Yes, exactly! This war

was always wrong. The South Vietnamese never did have any commitment to it."

Rick knew that, of course, but he looked at her for a long time before he finally said, "Judy, it's not that simple."

Her face changed. Some of the old hardness returned. "Oh, and you know that because you've *been* there. Right?"

"No. I don't know everything. But you don't have any idea what it's like."

"I know we're napalming villages and killing children. I know that our soldiers are turning into heartless killers. Everyone knows about Calley's massacre at My Lai, but there's a lot more of the same kind of stuff going on. This is the most evil war in history, Rick, so *don't* start defending it."

Judy knew some stuff. But she didn't know Trang. She didn't know Whiley or J. D. either. How could she claim to know about the war without knowing them? And how could he tell her? "Judy, it's not . . ." He wasn't sure how to say it. "It's not an *idea*. Do you know what I mean?"

"No, I don't."

He wasn't sure what he'd meant either. But the thought had been in his head for a long time. "The mistake of this war has always been the same. We thought an idea was more important than the people."

"That's what I've been telling you from the beginning.

But tell the whole truth, Rick. I hear how sick our soldiers are—how they walk around with 'born to kill' written on their helmets. You can't tell me that doesn't happen. The papers are reporting that stuff all the time."

"The soldiers are some of the people I'm talking about. They're victims too."

"Yes, that's right. Listen, why don't you come up to Berkeley and speak at one of our rallies? It would be so great if you would tell people that."

Rick was astounded. She didn't understand at all. Had she even bothered to try?

Judy was actually looking excited. "You could be a powerful spokesman for the vets against the war."

Rick got up. He had to get away. "I'm not an idea either, Judy," he said.

"What?"

"Our soldiers are heroes, whether you'll ever understand that or not."

She let her eyes roll back in a little motion of dismissal. "Oh, come on, Rick. They may be victims. I can buy that. But don't call them heroes."

"Would you die for me?"

"Die for you? What's that supposed to mean?"

"I saw some beautiful things over there, Judy—along with all the destruction. That's what people at home don't know."

"Guys dying for other guys—when they shouldn't be dying at all? Don't tell me that's beautiful."

"Like I said, you wouldn't understand." Rick took a few steps toward the door. "It was good to see you."

But then he heard her ask, "Why did you come over here if you don't want to talk about it?"

He stopped and turned back. He'd thought about that. "I just wanted to see you. You said you'd write to me, but you didn't."

"I was going to. But I didn't know what to say, so I kept putting it off—and then you came back so fast. I didn't think that would happen."

"Fast?" Rick tried to think what she meant. That last night he'd seen her, before he left, was part of a childhood he could only vaguely remember.

"I guess it doesn't seem fast to you."

"No."

He saw the recognition in her face, a hint of shame, and he was reminded how pretty she was. Her hair was resting on her shoulders, touching the skin that her sun dress didn't cover.

"We were really close at one time," he said. "I've been wondering since I got back if maybe things had changed. You know, maybe we could be like that again."

He saw her sadness deepen. "We're just too different, Rick."

"Yeah." He tried to smile. "Well, I wanted to say hello. I hope things turn out good for you."

She looked away from a moment, and then looked him in the eye again. "Rick, I dated a guy this last year.

He was interesting. But I never felt anything for him like I felt for you. I think that kind of thing only happens once, when you're young and you fall in love for the first time."

He nodded once, then nodded again. "Probably so." He started for the door.

"Call me once in a while, okay? Come and see me this summer, before I go back to school."

He opened the door. "No," he said. "I don't think so." He could see that she was confused, but he didn't know how to explain. He still cared for her too much just to hang around with her once in a while.

He walked on out to his mother's car, got in, and started the engine. He'd realized, talking to Judy, what he really needed to do. He'd heard from Kent, who was back home in Idaho now. He'd wanted to talk to him; now he needed to.

He drove home. He waited until his mother said she was going to the grocery store, and then he called long distance—even though his father would be upset about the bill that would show up. Kent's mother answered the phone; she sounded just the way Rick would have expected. Then Kent came on the line. He sounded almost overwhelmed. It had been so long since they had talked.

"Rick, how are you doing?"

"Okay. Better than you, I'd guess." He laughed a little too hard.

"Hey, I doubt that. I'm in great shape."

"You are? Really?" Rick sat down at the kitchen table.

"Sure. I walk around like anyone else. Most people never know that I lost my foot."

"That's good, Kent. That's really good. I'm doing great too. I'm way too skinny right now, but I can fix that."

"I got a letter from Whiley," Kent said.

"You did?"

"Yeah. I didn't know he could write." They both laughed. "It was a mixed-up letter, I'll tell you, but he told me about giving you the money for Trang."

"Yeah, he did. Sixty dollars."

"*Sixty!* He didn't tell me that."

"He had a Vietnamese nurse. I think that changed how he thought about some things."

"He said you saved his life."

"All of us did. But he's pretty busted up inside. I guess he told you that, too."

"Yeah. And he told me about J. D."

"Yeah."

Rick looked down at the tabletop—a pattern of gray and silver in an old chrome set that Mom and Dad had had forever. Dad had made him sit there when he was little and didn't want to finish the food on his plate. Rick had stared at the table then, too.

"Are you really okay, Rick? You sound a little upset."

"Well, it's been kind of hard—you know, the adjustment and everything. Being home. My dad's still . . . I don't know, Kent. I'm nervous, and I've been having dreams. It's hard for me to sit around the house and . . ." But he couldn't talk anymore. His voice was about to come apart. His whole head was.

"Rick, I know. We all know. At the hospital, I've talked to a lot of guys. It's bad for a while. But we'll be okay."

Rick concentrated on his breathing. He kept it steady, and he didn't talk. But it was good to think that Kent might be right.

"Are you still there?"

"Yeah." Rick took another breath, and then he said, "I was wondering if I could maybe come up there to Idaho. I'd just like to . . . you know . . . get together and talk some things over."

"That'd be great, Rick. I'd like to do that. You can stay with us. We've got plenty of room."

"Okay. I'm not sure when. But I'll figure something out."

"Are you planning to start school this fall?"

"Maybe. I've thought about that. I could use my G. I. Bill money."

"That's right. That's a good idea."

"What if I came up to Utah State? I've thought a little bit about that. You said in your letter you might go back there this fall."

"That's right. You told me I wasn't cut out to be a farmer, and I'm not. Especially a one-legged farmer. I'm going to go to grad school. I need a doctorate if I'm going to be a professor, but for now, I got accepted into a master's program. If I make up my mind to go beyond that, I might even try to go off to some big-name school."

"But you *will* be there this fall?"

"Definitely."

"Is it too late for me to apply, or—"

"No. You can still get in. I've been looking for an apartment or maybe a house. I've got a friend who wants to share the rent. But if you came up here, that would reduce the bill for all of us. I'd really like that."

"I'd only be a freshman, and you guys would be way ahead of me."

"What difference does that make?"

"I don't know. I'm just trying to think about every-thing. I can't seem to make decisions lately."

"We don't have the army to make them for us."

"That's right."

They laughed again. Rick felt a little better. But he was still nervous. He put his hand flat on the table, to keep it from shaking.

"What are you thinking you might study?" Kent asked.

"That's something else I don't know for sure. Maybe I still want to be a writer."

"I thought you changed your mind, back in Nam."

"I did. But lately I've been thinking about it again."

"You could write about some of your experiences in the war."

Rick stood up suddenly and his chair scraped across the linoleum. "No. I don't want to do that."

"So what would you write about?"

"I'm not really sure. But I want to say something about people looking out for each other. I've been writing in my notebook once in a while, and I've got some ideas. I've got to work a lot more on the plot and everything."

"That's good, Rick. You'd be a good man to write about that kind of stuff."

Rick wondered. He hoped he was good. And he hoped he was a man. He'd gone to Vietnam to find out who he was, but he had come home still unclear about that. What he did know was that he liked himself best when he was around Kent, and Kent was definitely a good man.

"Kent, I went back to the platoon before I came home. I told them that Whiley had given me that sixty dollars, and how you'd sent some more. The men were really surprised about Whiley, but almost all of them chipped in after they heard what you two had done. I took more than a hundred and fifty bucks to Trang and Vo Thi. She cried, she was so happy. She even put her arms around me."

"That's great, Rick. I can hardly believe those guys would do that."

"I know. I think it's the best I ever felt—when the men in the platoon gave me the money, and then when I gave it to Trang."

"I know what you're saying."

"I just hope the war ends now, and everyone comes out all right—Trang and Vo Thi and all the guys we knew over there."

"Yeah. And everyone else in Vietnam."

Again there was silence, but Rick didn't want to hang up. He was calming down, feeling much better.

"So when are you coming up here?"

"I don't know. As soon as I can work everything out."

"Good." Rick was trying to think what else to say when Kent added, "We'll be all right, Rick. We were down, but we're not out."

"Yeah. I think that's right, Kent."

"We'll get up off the mat and score a knockout."

"Naw. We don't need to win. Let's use your method. Let's just love everyone who knocked us down. They won't know how to handle that."

Kent laughed long and hard. "That's right," he said. "That's what we need to do. We just might end the whole fight."

"And all the ones that come after it."

This time there was a very long silence, and then Kent said. "I wish it were that simple. It really ought to be."

Rick took another long breath. "Yeah. That's what I've been thinking."

NOTE ON SOURCES

I have read dozens of books on war—on Vietnam and especially on reconnaissance units. The following books are some of the ones I've consulted (note that they are not books for young readers and most contain adult material):

Baker, Mark. *Nam: The Vietnam War in the Words of the Men and Women Who Fought There*. New York: Cooper Square Press, 2001.

Caputo, Philip. *A Rumor of War: With a Twentieth Anniversary Postscript by the Author*. New York: Henry Holt & Co., 1996.

Chambers, Larry. *Death in the A Shau Valley: L Company LRRPs in Vietnam, 1969–70*. New York: Ivy Books, 1998.

Hedges, Chris. *War is the Force That Gives Us Meaning*. New York: PublicAffairs, 2002.

Herr, Michael. *Dispatches*. New York: Vintage Books, 1991.

Hess, Gary R. *Vietnam and the United States: Origins and Legacy of War.* Boston: Twayne Publishers, 1990.

Karnow, Stanley. *Vietnam: A History.* New York: Viking Press, 1983.

Ketwig, John. *—And a Hard Rain Fell: A GI's True Story of the War in Vietnam.* New York: Collier Macmillan, 1985.

Jorgenson, Kregg P. J. *Acceptable Loss.* New York: Ivy Books, 1991.

Laurence, John. *The Cat from Hué: A Vietnam War Story.* New York: PublicAffairs, 2002.

Leppelman, John. *Blood on the Risers: An Airborne Soldiers Thirty-five Months in Vietnam.* New York: Ivy Books, 1991.

Linderer, Gary A. *The Eyes of the Eagle.* New York: Ivy Books, 1991.

_____. *Six Silent Men: 101st LRP/Rangers.* New York: Ivy Books, 1997.

_____. *Phantom Warriors.* New York: Ballantine Books, 2000.

McDonald, Cherokee Paul. *Into the Green: A Reconnaissance by Fire.* New York: Plume, 2001.

Moore, Harold G. *We Were Soldiers Once . . . And Young: Ia Drang, the Battle That Changed the War in Vietnam.* New York: Ballantine Books, 2004.

Ogden, Richard E. *Green Knight, Red Mourning.* New York: Zebra Books, 1985.

O'Nan, Stewart, ed. *The Vietnam Reader: The Definitive Collection of American Fiction and Nonfiction on the War.* New York: Anchor Books, 1998.

Parker, Jr., James E. *Covert Ops: The CIA's Secret War in Laos*. New York: St. Martin's Paperbacks, 1995.

Puller, Lewis B. *Fortunate Son: The Autobiography of Lewis B. Puller Jr.* New York: Grove Weidenfeld, 1991.

Rotundo, John L. and Don Ericson. *Charlie Rangers*. New York: Ivy Books, 1988.

Sheehan, Neil. *A Bright Shining Lie: John Paul Vahn and American in Vietnam*. New York: Vintage, 1989.

Spector, Ronald H. *After Tet: The Bloodiest Year in Vietnam*. New York: Free Press, Maxwell Macmillan International, 1993.

If I may recommend one simple but stunning book that *everyone* should read, it is:

Hedges, Chris. *What Every Person Should Know About War*. New York: Free Press, 2003.